M
SHELTON, Connie

Small towns can be
murder

SMALL TOWNS CAN BE MURDER

by Connie Shelton

INTRIGUE
PRESS

    For information, please contact Intrigue Press, P.O. Box 456, Angel Fire,
NM 87710, 505-377-3474

    ISBN 1-890768-05-7

    First printing 1998

    This book is a work of fiction. Names, characters, places and incidents
are either the product of the author's imagination or are used fictitiously. Any
resemblance to actual events or locales or persons, living or dead, is entirely
coincidental. Although the author and publisher have made every effort to
ensure the accuracy and completeness of information contained in this book,
we assume no responsibility for errors, inaccuracies, omissions, or any incon-
sistency herein. Any slights of people, places, or organizations are uninten-
tional.

    Library of Congress Cataloging-in-Publication Data

Shelton, Connie.
    Small towns can be murder / Connie Shelton.
      p.   cm.
    ISBN 1-890768-05-7 (hardcover)
    I. Title.
    PS3569.H393637S63   1998
    813'.54--dc21   98-10454
                                                            CIP

For Dan, as always, my love and my inspiration. And to our own sweet Lady. Together we're the three musketeers.

Special thanks and appreciation to those without whom this book would not have happened: Dan Shelton for his steady support and strong shoulders; Gretchen Lemons for her insights into the workings of medical offices; Susan Samson and Mary Cimarolli-Robottom for careful editing and fixes to the plot; and finally to the members of the Moreno Valley Writers Guild, who provided much appreciated critiques.

1

New Mexico is a land of contrasts. Hidden deep within the Sangre de Cristo mountain range, from north of Santa Fe to the Colorado border are dozens of little secluded towns. Part of the old Camino Real, that legendary trading route between the settled world and the wild west, these quaint adobe enclaves hold tightly to their secrets. No matter how dirty.

Sally Bertrand and I were in my Jeep, driving north on I-25, just leaving the Santa Fe city limits. My name is Charlotte Louise Parker, a CPA by profession, partner with my brother, Ron, in a private investigation agency in Albuquerque. No one actually calls me Charlotte. I'm Charlie to everyone who knows me. Sally is our part-time receptionist and a good friend.

Sally had called me the night before, sounding blue. Her husband, Ross, had just found out he'd have to work this Fourth of July weekend, cancelling plans they'd made for a backpacking trip together. Ross works in construction and, with the recent slump in building, must have felt that he'd better take the work no matter when it came. Sally called to see if I'd be interested in taking his place on the trip. Loading a forty pound pack on my back and carrying it off to some spot that has neither toilet facilities nor take-out food ranks right up there in my book with stuffing matchsticks under my fingernails. Sally knows this and, as an alternative, suggested that we take the day off and drive north.

Sally's hometown of Valle Escondido is about ninety minutes out of Albuquerque, and does at least boast some paved streets and a few respectable Mexican restaurants. We arrived before noon, just in time to find a parking spot in front of Rosa's Cantina, where we ordered huevos rancheros smothered in green chile.

Once our waitress removed the menus, I took a minute to look around. We sat in one of three rooms with heavy hand-carved tables and chairs set at intervals with lots of space between them. The walls were of adobe, over two feet thick, brown on the outside, brightly whitewashed on the inside. Sturdy poles supported the roof made of vigas interlaced with narrow latillas. Long strands of red chile hung from the vigas on the outside of the building. We were spared the cuteness of miniature pinatas, gaudy serapes, or glittering velvet sombreros as wall decor.

Outside our window the street curved away, lined by rows of more adobe buildings, their rounded brown lines broken occasionally by dusty green trees. It was the main drag through town, having all the charm of Santa Fe or Taos, without the tourists. The two thousand residents apparently preferred it this way.

Sally's eyes traveled to the curve in the road and back, taking in sights familiar yet different.

"That bookstore over there?" She indicated a blue door across the street. "That's where I had my first after-school job. I was working there when Ross walked in and asked for a book on backpacking. I was two years out of high school when we met, and I think it was love at first sight."

Her eyes sparkled, and I felt a brief stab of almost-jealousy that she had found her soul mate at such a young age. My own love life had consisted of years of ups and downs, with one distinct possibility coming onto the scene during my Hawaiian vacation a couple of months ago. It reminded me that he'd be here for a visit within the week.

"Remember that park we passed on the way in?" Sally asked. "It used to be so *big*. Do all our childhood haunts shrink when we get older?"

I couldn't say. I still live in the house I grew up in, having inherited it after my parents were killed in a plane crash when I was a junior in high school. But I could see what Sally meant. I wondered what it was like for her, growing up in a small town like this.

Our huevos arrived just then. Using a potholder, the waitress set them down and warned us that the plates were hot. Waves of steam rose from the plate with the first cut of my fork. The chile, cheese, egg, beans, and tortilla steamed for a moment on the tines before I tentatively took a bite. Umm . . . heaven.

"So, how do you want to spend the day?" I asked, once Sally and I had both reached a stopping place.

"Well," she answered, "I thought about calling my friend Laura Armijo. The last I heard she was still living here."

She thought about that a minute, then chuckled. Sally lights up when she laughs. Otherwise, she's on the plain side — pear shaped body, small breasts, shaggy blond hair, a few freckles on an honest-looking face. Two weeks ago she learned that she's pregnant, something they'd been working on for months, and there does seem to be a little more glow surrounding her now.

"Actually, I couldn't imagine Laura living anywhere but here," she said. "Her parents and grandparents live here. Her great-grandchildren will probably live here."

"Did she know you were coming?"

"No. Obviously, *we* didn't even know we were coming. We'll just stop by her place after lunch."

I liked the informality of it. Right off hand, I couldn't think of a single friend I could just drop in on, other than my eighty-six year old neighbor, Elsa Higgins. Being with Sally today wasn't making me feel any better about my independence.

We had finished lunch and divided the check. Sally gave directions, and I guided my Jeep along the back streets she indicated.

Laura's house was a picture postcard. A huge cottonwood tree cast dappled shadows over the adobe house and the driveway. We parked in the shade in front of a tall wooden gate set deeply into an adobe wall. Lamps of Mexican wrought iron flanked the sides of the gate, and red chile ristras hung below the lamps. Someone had planted flowers along the front of the wall, bright orange-red geraniums and tall purple cosmos. The gate itself was heavy wood weathered into a gray plank of deep crevices. The pungent scent of roasting chile filled the air.

Sally pushed the gate open, and we stepped into a spacious courtyard. Here, the same attention to detail was evident. Pots of geraniums lined the walkway. A small *horno*, an adobe bread oven, was built into one corner of the courtyard. Black soot stains around the opening indicated that the oven was not merely decorative. The flagstone walk had been recently washed, the gravel areas around it freshly raked. Being somewhat of a neatness fanatic myself, I found the whole place immensely appealing.

The house was built in a U shape, flanking three sides of the courtyard. As I scanned the area, trying to determine which would be the front door, a woman came out, her step questioning and tentative. She was petite, with dark hair cut short and stylish, and skin the color of coffee with a lot of cream added. She wore jeans and a plaid shirt with the sleeves rolled up. She stopped just under the edge of the covered portal.

"Sally!" It was almost a shriek as she flew down the walkway toward us.

Laura disappeared into Sally's big hug. They exclaimed over each other for a good three minutes before either of them realized I was standing there shifting from one foot to the other.

"Where are my manners?" Sally said, turning to me. "Charlie, this is my old friend, Laura."

Laura was just as welcoming to me as she had been to Sally. Her smile was infectious, showing straight white teeth, and well-defined smile wrinkles at both sides of her mouth. She took my hand and led us both toward the house.

"Let's sit out here," she said. "It's cooler. I've been roasting chile all morning."

A round glass-topped table stood in one corner of the patio. We pulled out the cushioned chairs around it and sat down.

"Can I get you something to drink?" Laura asked. "Tea, Cokes, anything?"

I was still full from the meal we'd just eaten, but Laura seemed determined to be a good hostess. Sally and I both opted for iced tea. Laura was gone only a couple of minutes before she came back with tall glasses of tea with lemon slices floating on top. She also brought a plate of cinnamon and sugar covered bizcochitos, a cookie I've never been able to resist. I proceeded to munch down two of them while Sally and Laura caught up on their news.

Laura was thrilled to hear about Sally's pregnancy.

"Aren't you and Bobby about ready to try again?" Sally asked.

"No, not yet." Laura's voice was hesitant. Her dark eyes stared out toward the small patch of lawn in the middle of the courtyard.

Sally reached over and took her hand. "Losing one baby isn't the end of the world," she said. "That was three years ago."

"I know," said Laura. "It scares me, though, to want something so much." She wiped the moisture from her tea glass with a napkin. Her hands and eyes stayed busy as she spoke. "Maybe it's better for now to stick with my job at the bank. We're putting a little money aside, you know, finally getting a little ahead."

The back screen door opened just then, pushed slowly outward by an elderly woman. She spoke to Laura rapidly in Spanish, with Laura answering the same way. The old woman nodded briefly toward Sally and me, then ducked back inside.

"My husband's grandmother," Laura explained. "There's a phone call for me."

She glanced around the patio. A phone stood on a small table near the door. "I must have turned the ringer off on this one," she said. She walked to it and picked up the receiver.

"Hello? Hi, Richard, what's up?"

I had no intention of listening to the phone call, but there was no way I could avoid it. My chair faced the spot where Laura stood, and she made no effort to conceal either the caller or the content. As I watched, the color drained from her face.

"No!" she screamed. "Oh my God, no!"

Her hand went to her mouth, and her knees began to give way. Sally and I both were out of our chairs in an instant. Tears were streaming down Laura's face by the time she hung up the phone. Sally held her close, while I stood by feeling completely useless and very much out of place. Laura's sobs built in intensity before beginning to subside.

Sally held her at arm's length at last.

"What is it, Laura?" she asked gently.

"My friend, Cynthia," she choked. "She's dead."

2

Laura's legs threatened to give way again. Sally steered her toward her chair.

"What happened?" I finally had the courage to ask. Perhaps talking about it would help her cope.

She took a sip of her tea and a little color came back into her face. I handed her a fresh napkin to wipe her cheeks. The tears had begun to dry in two salty tracks.

"Richard said she lost the baby." Her voice was tiny and not at all solid.

I glanced up at Sally. Her own face had gone white, her light freckles standing out vividly now. She flopped heavily into her chair. Her own pregnancy was still too new and fragile to take for granted. Being thirty years old was an added risk, and she knew it.

Laura was beginning to come around a little. Her fingers stayed busy folding the edges of her paper napkin into neat patterns.

"I don't know whether you knew Cynthia," she said to Sally. "She's a bit older than us."

Sally shook her head. She still hadn't spoken.

"Cynthia just turned thirty-seven," Laura continued. "She was so excited about this baby. You know, she lost one last year, and figured this might be her only chance to try again."

Tears puddled at the bottoms of her big brown eyes once more.

"Maybe we should go," I suggested gently.

Sally looked disoriented, but Laura pulled herself together. "No, please," she said. "I think I'd like company for awhile yet. At least until Bobby gets home." She looked over at Sally. "I could use a little help in the kitchen," she suggested.

We followed her into the house, and through a cool, dark dining room to the kitchen. A large skylight in the middle of the room made it light and airy feeling. Copper pots hung from hooks above a center work island. The counter tops were brightly patterned Mexican tiles in blue, rust, and yellow. The smell of roasted chile was prevalent. A shallow pan of green chile pods, their skins crispy from the broiler, sat atop the stove.

"Will you stay for dinner tonight?" Laura asked. "I was just going to make enchiladas."

I thought of the big meal we'd just eaten, and started to decline. But I looked toward Sally first. Maybe she needed this time with her friend.

"We better not," she said. "We had planned to drive back to Albuquerque this afternoon."

"Well, can you stay and help me make the sauce, anyway?"

We agreed and went to the sink to wash our hands. The next twenty minutes passed quietly as we peeled and chopped the roasted chiles, then chopped onions, garlic, and tomatoes for the sauce. Laura busied herself at the stove stirring the stock, adding each ingredient as we had it ready. Finally, there was nothing to do but let it simmer. The work had been therapeutic, though. Both Laura and Sally looked more stable.

Laura picked up the tea pitcher and pulled a tray of ice from the freezer.

"Let's go back outside and finish our tea," she suggested.

"Tell us about Cynthia," I encouraged. The sooner she could talk about it, the sooner she could work through the grief.

"She was my supervisor at the bank," Laura said. "Such a nice lady. She had lived next door to my mother, and we were friends for a long time. She helped me get the bank job."

"She and her husband were really looking forward to the baby, I guess?"

"I know she was. Richard's a funny guy. I have a hard time knowing what he thinks." Something in her expression closed down, warning me that she didn't want to talk about Richard.

She decided to check the sauce on the stove just then, leaving Sally and me alone on the patio.

"What do you think about that?" Sally asked in a whisper.

"The way Laura closed up about Richard just now? You mean like she and he . . ."

"No! Laura is a hundred percent devoted to Bobby. I mean she almost acted like she was afraid of Richard."

Through the screen I could see Laura heading back toward us, so I motioned Sally to silence. Laura's face was still preoccupied when she sat down. I glanced back at Sally. She raised her eyebrows in a questioning way. Okay, I can ask a painful question or two.

"Laura, I got the feeling you don't like Richard too much," I prompted.

She turned in her chair, facing now out into the yard, her expression flittering through a variety of emotions.

"Charlie's a private investigator," Sally told her. "Maybe she can help if there's a problem."

Laura started to say something.

"I'm not really a private investigator," I told her. "I'm a partner in an investigation firm. Occasionally I get pulled into something where I can ask a few questions and help figure out some answers."

"She's good," Sally piped in. "Just last month she caught a murderer."

I waved my hand toward her, hoping she wouldn't go into a lot of detail. The occasion had prompted an on-going argument with my brother about my refusal to use a handgun. I've always been opposed to them, but he has quite stubbornly and reasonably pointed out that I came pretty close to getting myself killed a month ago, and that I better learn to protect myself. I'm not convinced yet. At least I'm not ready to admit anything to him.

Laura was looking at me with a new expression on her face. I wasn't exactly sure how to interpret it.

"Do you know how to get information from people?" she asked. "I mean, like police reports and things?"

"Sometimes." I waited. She chewed her lower lip.

"If I tell you something, you have to promise, and I mean a deadly serious promise, that you won't say anything."

"Laura, that would depend on what you tell me. There are some things I'd have to report."

"Then, could you not tell anyone where you heard it? I mean, this is a small town."

"Again, that depends." Why wouldn't she just come out with it?

She leaned closer, her voice a whisper this time. Sally and I found ourselves leaning forward, too.

"I think Richard used to beat Cynthia," she said.

That said, we all leaned back in our chairs once again.

"Did Cynthia ever tell you this?" I asked.

"Oh, no." Denial was quick and firm. "Maybe I shouldn't have said anything."

I kept my gaze level. "Laura, if you know your friend was being abused, you have to say so. Do you think Richard's abuse might have caused Cynthia's miscarriage?"

"I don't know." Her face closed.

Sally reached over to take her friend's hand. She squeezed it while she addressed me. "Charlie, there's something you may not understand." She looked again at Laura, sending reassurance through her fingertips. "Women around here don't talk about things like that."

My jaw must have dropped, because she went on.

"They just don't." She fixed her eyes on mine. Meaning, Hispanic women around here don't talk about these things. I got her meaning, and tried to be gentle with my next question.

"What made you think Richard was beating his wife?" I asked.

Again, Laura looked away briefly, unable to say it right out. "One time Cynthia came to work with a black eye," she said quietly. "She said she had bumped into the door. I knew it wasn't true. After that, he was more careful. She must have said something to him. Once I saw an ugly bruise mark on her arm and I asked her about it. After that, she wore long sleeves all the time." She sipped her tea and took a deep breath. "Once, she opened a file drawer a little too fast and it hit her in the belly. She almost screamed with the pain. Then she acted confused, and said that she'd had a stomach ache all day anyway. I never came out and asked her about any of it. It's just one of those things you know without asking."

"Do you think she would have reported this to the police?"

"If she wouldn't even tell a good friend?"

"How about a doctor? Were any of the injuries bad enough to need a doctor?"

"I don't know. There's only the one clinic in town. She would have had to go there." Again, a pause for another sip of tea.

"Cynthia Martinez was a good woman. She didn't deserve that kind of treatment, Charlie."

Sally spoke up. "It just seems odd to me, in this day and time, for a woman to die from a miscarriage. I don't know, maybe it still happens, but . . ."

The unfinished sentence dangled in the air between the three of us.

3

"Would it be a problem for you to stay overnight?" Sally asked the question as we drove out of Laura's narrow lane.

Something in her voice got my attention just before the words of refusal came to my lips. I glanced at her out of the corner of my eye. Her blue eyes were wide, her mouth set with a tension I'd seldom seen. Suddenly the question was important.

"I suppose I could," I answered neutrally. "What do you have in mind?" As if I didn't know.

She didn't speak for a minute. When she did, there were tears in her voice. "Charlie, what's the matter with me? I didn't even know Cynthia Martinez. But, somehow I desperately care about what happened to her. Do you suppose we could stay around awhile and look into it?"

"Sure. Let's find a room for the night, then we'll phone home so nobody worries." Even as I said it, I realized that as long as I could get my neighbor to feed my dog and let him out, there was no one home to worry about me. "Will Ross mind your staying?"

"Oh, no. Not for one night. He'll be working anyway."

We stopped at a small variety store that was about to close early because it was Sunday afternoon. We each picked out toothbrushes, toothpaste, and an oversize t-shirt to sleep in. At home I sleep in the nude, but felt a little funny about it in the same room with Sally. Although she's a friend, she's also an employee. We decided we could rinse out our undies in the sink and wear the same clothes tomorrow.

The Ponderosa Inn had a vacancy. Despite the fact that this was a holiday weekend, obviously Valle Escondido was not crowded with vacationers. It just isn't your destination kind of town. The room was clean, but stiflingly hot. We opened the door and cranked the air conditioner all the way up. Within a few minutes, it became bearable. For our twenty-three dollars, we'd rented two double beds with equally saggy-looking mattresses, towels only slightly thicker than the sheets, and a view of the parking lot. Heat waves rose off the blacktop, so we closed the door.

"Now what?" Sally asked after we had each called home. My neighbor, Elsa Higgins, had been more than glad to take Rusty in for the night, no questions asked. Ross, as predicted, was easy-going about whatever Sally wanted to do.

"I guess that's up to you," I told her. "Did you just want to hang out, or did you have in mind that we try to get to the bottom of the situation with Cynthia?"

She squirmed a little, knowing that I'm a sucker for the underdog, and have at times risked my own life to prove a point.

"Well... I was kind of thinking we could ask a few questions," she said.

Actually, I had been thinking the same thing myself. "Okay," I said, "you're the native. Tell me if anyone you know around here might help us."

She looked a little blank. We stretched out on our beds to think.

"Well," I continued, "we should find out where she died. If she was home, who else was there? If she went to the hospital, who was her doctor? If there was anything suspicious about the death, there might have been a police report filed."

"Like I told Laura, I didn't know Cynthia when I lived here. As far as I can remember, I didn't know her family, although it's a pretty good bet that a third of this town is named Martinez."

I picked up the phone book from the nightstand between us, and thumbed through the pages while she talked. There were two Richard Martinezes listed, one Rick, and two others with the initial R.

"There isn't a hospital here, only the clinic. But I think I do know one of the doctors there," she said brightening somewhat.

"Would they be around on a Sunday afternoon?" I asked.

"Umm . . . Not likely. And tomorrow's a holiday." She sounded disappointed at this revelation.

"But there must be a number people use for emergencies. One of the doctors must be on call."

"Probably," she agreed.

"Why don't we take a little drive, get some dinner, and you can show me around the town? I'd like to get my bearings."

The late afternoon sun was still high in the cloudless sky. It had been more than a month since the last rain, and the brown-tinged grass and droopy shrubs showed it. Even the ponderosa pines were grayish in the heat. It would probably be another month before the seasonal rains began. This is the time of year when sprinkler systems work overtime. The heat waves in the parking lot were intense. Even so, it was at least ten degrees cooler here than in Albuquerque. I was glad I'd pulled my shoulder length hair up into a ponytail and worn light cotton clothing.

Valle Escondido has one main street, and I had already seen most of it. The town sits at the opening to a small valley surrounded by mountains. There is only one way in. The road eventually runs out at the base of the hills. Coming into town from the south, we had passed a lumber yard, two car dealers, a motorcycle repair shop, and other service-type establishments. Our motel was next, followed by the small shopping center where we'd visited the variety store already. The center also housed a grocery store of respectable size, and two fast food places. Across the street from the grocery store was the clinic. Just past that, a turn-off to a small plaza. We circled it. The bustle and glamour of Santa Fe's plaza were entirely missing here. A few tired-looking trees stood in the middle of the square, the grass beneath them worn away and untended now. The buildings—a hotel, dry goods store, cafe, and saddlery—looked sadly unused. Their exteriors were shabby compared to the newer buildings in town.

Small side streets led to residential areas. Now Sally directed me to drive north. We passed Rosa's where we had eaten lunch. Beyond the curve in the road the businesses thinned. A fairly major side street led to the high school. Sally directed me to turn there, and we cruised the parking lot so she could reminisce. Out here the residences became larger. This must be the right side of town. Eventually these, too, petered out, the land becoming flatter. Farms with a few horses, cows, and sheep dotted the countryside. Beyond the flat land the mountains rose sharply, defining without question the hidden valley the place was named for.

Backtracking into town once again, we decided on a small diner that looked reasonably clean and comfortingly crowded. As we got out of the car, Sally pointed out the town government building across the street. It was a one-story adobe, like most everything else in town, and housed the mayor's office and police department. She thought they had probably a half dozen officers by now.

The diner served regular down-home style cookin' according to their sign. The chicken fried steak came with cream gravy, mashed potatoes, and a spoonful of canned green beans. Pretty much the way Elsa makes it "down-home." Sally had a large salad, lean turkey, and milk because of her condition. I knew it wouldn't hurt me to follow her example, but the chicken fried steak looked so much better. Again, I vowed to start an exercise routine soon.

"So, when does Drake arrive?" she asked, once we were working on our dinners.

"Next weekend," I answered.

Drake Langston was the helicopter pilot I'd met while on vacation in Hawaii a couple of months ago. He lives there and has, on more than one occasion, suggested that I join him. It's tempting. I'm just not sure I want to pack up and move three thousand miles away to be with a guy I've known mostly over the telephone. He's been extremely patient with my uncertainty so far. His upcoming vacation was meant to be an experiment in finding out how well we really do get along.

"Bet you can hardly wait," Sally continued. "I'd be on pins and needles to see him again."

"I guess I am kinda nervous about it," I admitted. "It's strange, thinking about him actually being here, staying at my house and all."

"Why? You stayed at his house when you went there," she reasonably pointed out.

"Only the last couple of days. After I got bashed over the head, and the doctor said I had to either stay in the hospital or have someone watch over me." I really hadn't admitted to Sally or anyone yet, just how close I'd come to falling in love with Drake during that ten day trip. I pride myself on being more level-headed than that. But his sexy smile had made an impression on me that holds to this day. The reminder of his tender lovemaking did have my insides fluttering again at the prospect of more.

I caught Sally trying to read my face.

"So," I said, changing the subject, "you mentioned that you know one of the doctors at the clinic? Well enough to ask some questions about Cynthia?"

"I can try. You know how doctors are about confidentiality, though. We may not learn a thing."

She was right. I was beginning to seriously question what we thought we might learn about a woman we didn't even know, who may or may not have died under perfectly normal circumstances.

Back in the room, I again picked up the phone book. There weren't that many Richard Martinezes listed, and I could think of only one way to find out which was our man.

I dialed the first number. "Is Cynthia there?" I asked.

4

The first two calls resulted in wrong number responses. My third such request met with anguished silence. In the background I could hear voices, like a house full of people milling around. I hung up.

"What's the custom here?" I asked Sally. "Do people come to the family home and bring food and all that?"

She nodded emphatically. "Definitely."

I read off the street name from the phone book. She knew where it was. "What do you think? Shall we mingle?"

The house on Vallejo Road was easy to spot by the number of cars around it. The late summer sun cast a golden light over the boxy little house, softening and hiding the cracks in the plaster and the peeling paint on the trim. Long shadows filled the yard. The heat had abated somewhat, and I noticed that most of the doors and windows stood open.

"If you see anyone you know, introduce me," I told Sally.

Inside, the house was like an oven. The first person we saw was Laura Armijo. She looked surprised to see us here, but didn't say anything about it. She introduced us to her husband, Bobby, a good-looking man of average height with jet black hair and eyes to match.

"Have you heard anything more about how it happened?" I asked Laura. We had moved off to a corner, keeping our voices low.

"They say she lost the baby, and the doctor couldn't make her stop bleeding," Laura said. "She just had a doctor's appointment Friday morning. She came to work late and started hemorrhaging badly that afternoon. Someone called an ambulance, but I guess it was too late." Her eyes brimmed.

"How far along was she?" I asked.

"Four months, I think."

"Anyone talking about . . . what we discussed earlier?"

She shook her dark head. "Not here, anyway." She pointed across the small living room. "That's Richard. Standing in the corner."

Sally and I had become separated somehow, and I glanced around to find her talking with an older blond woman near the doorway to the kitchen. She introduced the woman as Mrs. Green, her sixth grade teacher. Their conversation seemed to be an attempt to cover about fifteen years worth of "how've you been lately," so I meandered toward Richard's corner of the room.

The crowd seemed at a loss for what to do next. People stood in little clumps, not moving, speaking only in hushed tones and sobs. Shock was evident on every face. I watched Richard for several minutes before approaching him. He was a tall man with wavy black hair, thick lashes over deep brown eyes, and a pencil thin mustache. He wore a pale blue dress shirt open at the collar, with the sleeves rolled up. There were damp circles under the arms. His eyes were red rimmed, his hair disheveled like he had run his fingers through it several times. He took frequent pulls from a Budweiser can in his hand.

Another man, about the same age, but shorter and stockier than Richard stood by him. He sipped at a beer, too, and the two of them kept a steady conversation going except when interrupted by the sympathizers in the crowded room. Richard maintained his control pretty well, but occasionally emotion would register strongly on his face. The emotion I saw there was anger.

Gradually, as the people shifted about the room, I worked my way over to him. He gave brief acknowledgement to each person who spoke to him. I was curious to see what reaction I would get.

"Richard, I'm so very sorry," I said, extending my hand to him. "Such a shock this is."

"Yes," he said. His voice was softer than I expected.

I wanted to ask questions, but knew I was already drawing curiosity from both Richard and his companion. Surely they were wondering who the hell I was. Questions from me would certainly draw questions from them. I moved on.

At least I was getting a look at the potential adversary first hand. I could learn more by watching Richard's face and body language than by asking him direct questions at this point anyway. Sally was still engaged in her conversation with Mrs. Green, so I casually wandered through the room.

The house was quite small, I realized, and jammed with people. The living room formed an L with an insignificant dining room, where the table was crammed with covered dishes, molded gelatins, and cakes. Someone had found the plates and forks, and set up an impromptu buffet, but few at this point were partaking. Through a door was the kitchen, the counters littered with the foil wrappings from the various food dishes. Otherwise, it appeared neat and clean.

On the pretense of looking for the bathroom, I stepped into a hallway, from which I could see into two bedrooms and the bath, all at once. One of the rooms had obviously been planned as the baby's room. Pastel prints hung on the walls, a white crib stood in one corner. Perhaps Cynthia had decorated this room when she was pregnant the first time a year ago, saving it now for this baby which would never come. My throat closed up slightly at the thought.

The other bedroom was obviously the master. A double bed, unmade, stood in the center of one wall. A dresser with a portable TV set on top was across from it. A woman's hairbrush lay on the nightstand. Clothes were strewn over a chair. I stepped into the room. A handful of coins lay scattered over the carpet. The alarm clock lay on its side. Disorderly, but did they necessarily indicate a struggle? It was almost as though Cynthia had gotten up this morning, leaving Richard in bed, her nightgown draped over the back of a chair. She would make the bed and tidy the room later. Only she hadn't.

A framed photograph of Cynthia stood on the dresser. She had been in her late twenties or early thirties when the picture was taken. I was startled at how beautiful she'd been. Long dark hair fell in soft curls below her shoulders. Full lips, high cheekbones in a slim face, eyes the color of a chocolate bar, rimmed with elegant lashes. Hard to imagine why a man would want to hit her.

Both bedrooms were dark and quiet, and I didn't want to be caught snooping. I ducked in and pretended to use the bathroom, then nonchalantly worked my way back through the crowd in the living room. Sally looked relieved to see my face.

"I wondered where you'd gone," she said. "The last time I saw you, you were shaking hands with Richard."

I held up the hand, showing it to her. "Look, it's not even broken."

She shot me a look.

"Okay, okay. I'm ready to leave if you are," I suggested.

The cars out front had thinned a bit. The sun had set, but it was not yet pitch dark. We tucked into our room for the night. I switched on the TV for company and Sally pulled out a mystery she'd brought along.

"What are you reading?"

She held it up so I could see the cover. "*Whose Death Is It, Anyway?* by Elizabeth Daniels Squire. She has this older woman sleuth who can never remember anything. It's hilarious."

I left her chuckling over some passage in the book while I flipped channels on the TV. Nothing held my attention. Somehow, I couldn't forget that empty nursery.

5

The sun was bright, the sky cloudless by the time we opened our curtains the next morning. It would be another warm day. July 4th. I didn't have much hope of finding a doctor in his office, but we had decided to try. With one clinic in town, three doctors on staff, surely someone must be around, even on holidays.

There were three cars in the clinic's parking lot, a dusty gray compact with a small dent in the right front fender, a snappy blue sports car, and a brand new four-wheel drive Suburban. It was a pretty easy guess which one did not belong to a doctor. We parked next to it.

The clinic itself was a more modern looking structure than most of the buildings in town. It was stuccoed the obligatory adobe brown, however it did have a contemporary image. A carved wooden sign beside the walkway announced the doctors' names: Evan Phillips, Rodney Phillips, Brent Fisher. They all had groups of letters after their names, Evan Phillips boasting the most.

"I went to school with Rod Phillips," Sally told me. "Should have known he'd end up in practice with his older brother. There's been a Dr. Phillips in this town since anyone can remember. I think they pass the title down through the generations."

"No Spanish surname doctors? I thought this town was predominantly Hispanic."

"Actually it's about half Hispanic, half Anglo," she said. "As for the doctors, I don't know. Guess it's just timing. There was a doctor Hidalgo when I was a kid. He and Rod's father had their offices in a little place just off the plaza. This clinic was built about the time I was in high school."

We pushed through the glass entry doors, passing a tall slim man on his way out. He nodded politely without smiling, smoothed his blond hair with one hand, and headed toward the blue sports car. A sleepy-looking receptionist sat behind the front desk, sipping coffee from a styrofoam cup. She covered a yawn when she spotted us, then smiled apologetically.

She was the kind of girl everyone always said "she has such a pretty face" about. Twenty-three or -four years old, she was a good hundred pounds overweight. Her light brown hair was cut extremely short, giving the impression that her head was much too small for her body. Her makeup was well done, though, emphasizing large blue eyes, which she must have seen as her best feature. She was right. Her name tag read: C. Smith.

The reception desk was a half oval of neutral beige Formica. It was cleared except for a six-line telephone, and a few mandatory office supplies such as stapler and tape dispenser. Oh, and the Dunkin' Donuts box and her coffee cup.

"May I help you?" she asked.

Since she was obviously not overloaded with work, I decided a cozy chat might be the best approach.

"They dragged you out pretty early for a holiday, huh?"

"Yeah, we switch off shifts for that. I'd lot rather do Fourth of July than Christmas, though. Jenny drew Christmas this year.

It's the pits, I'll tell you. Every little kid who gets a new bike manages to fall off it on Christmas day. I drew it last year. I swear, we had a cracked wrist, two broken fingers, and at least four bumps on the head that day.

"I'm sorry," she continued, "that's not what you came in for. It's just that neither of you look like a medical emergency. If you need to see the doctor, you just missed Dr. Fisher but Dr. Phillips is in. He's not busy." She looked past us to the bank of empty waiting room chairs.

"Oh, no, Miss Smith, we don't need to see a doctor," I assured her.

"Call me Chris," she said. "We're real informal here."

"Okay Chris." I gave her a real informal smile. "Neither of us has a medical problem. Actually, we were friends of Cynthia Martinez. We were so shocked to hear about her death. She was a patient here, wasn't she?"

"Everybody in town is," Chris answered.

"What happened, anyway?"

She hesitated a fraction of a second, glancing toward double doors that led to the innards of the clinic. There had been no sound or movement from that direction since we'd arrived.

"She had a miscarriage and died of extensive hemorrhaging."

"Isn't that kind of unusual nowadays?" I asked. "I mean, with modern technology and all?"

"Well, she was a little old to be having her first baby," Chris replied. She paused, realizing how that sounded. "I mean, she was older than most of our maternity patients. And she was already into her fourth month before she came in. Most of them are here the minute they suspect they're pregnant."

"She'd been pregnant once before, hadn't she? About a year ago?"

Chris wrinkled her eyebrows just a bit. "Yes, I think so. I don't remember that too well."

"Was she in here often? For other things, I mean."

She started to roll her chair backward toward the cabinets where the patient files were kept, but quickly realized that would definitely be breaking a confidence. "I really can't talk about a patient's medical history, you know."

"Oh, I know," I said, pretending that had been the furthest thing from my mind. "I wouldn't want you to do anything wrong. We were just worried about Cynthia." I dropped my voice to a murmur. "Another friend who worked with her told me she thought Cynthia's husband was abusive."

"Well, I can't come right out and confirm that," she murmured back at me, "but . . ."

The door from the inner hallway swung toward us just then, startling her into silence.

"Chris, I need . . . Oh, sorry. I didn't realize anyone was here."

The doctor was a good-looking man in his early thirties, about five-eleven, with curly brown hair a little on the longish side. He wore tortoise rimmed glasses. His white shirt was open at the collar, his tie loosened, the sleeves rolled up to reveal tan arms with a light growth of hair on them.

"Rod!" Sally exclaimed.

"Sally McConnell?" He lowered his clipboard and looked over the tops of his glasses at her.

"Well, it's Sally Bertrand now," she answered. "It's good to see you. You're here in practice now?"

He nodded, rocking slightly back on his heels. Then he glanced over at me.

"Oh, I'm sorry," Sally said. "This is my employer and friend from Albuquerque, Charlie Parker."

We shook hands. He had attractive brown eyes and a slight gap between his front teeth.

"Come on back," he invited. "We're not exactly overflowing with patients this morning, although later I expect the usual abundance of burned fingers and toes from the fireworks."

We passed several examining rooms before another hall branched off to the right. A sign indicated surgery. Probably minor out-patient procedures. Straight ahead was a closed door with the name Evan Phillips, MD on the door. Rod indicated a door on the left. His name was on it in the same gold letters. Across the hall from Rod's was another closed door — Brent Fisher, MD.

Medium brown commercial grade carpeting covered the floors in the halls and his private office. His furnishings consisted of a large desk with comfortable high backed chair, two side chairs, a wall of bookcases behind him, and a sofa against the far wall. All the upholstery was done in earth tones, popular about ten years ago. His walls were hung with framed diplomas, and a couple of southwestern art lithographs done by nobody famous. A framed photograph of a wife and baby stood on the bookcase, just at visitor eye-level when seated.

He apologized for the desktop, which was littered with files. He made an effort to straighten them while Sally and I sat down in the two beige side chairs.

"So, you're married now, living in Albuquerque, and what did you say you do?" he asked Sally.

"I work for Charlie and her brother. Charlie and I decided to take the holiday off and drive up here yesterday. That's when we heard about Cynthia Martinez."

"Oh, you knew Cynthia?"

"Well, not exactly. She was a co-worker with a friend of mine, Laura Armijo. We were at Laura's house yesterday when she got the news. She was very upset."

"Naturally. It was tragic." His voice was sympathetic.

"Laura thought Cynthia might have been an abused wife," I said. "She had seen a few suspicious instances."

"Well, of course, as her doctors, none of us could comment on that."

"But shouldn't the police be brought into it if her death might have been caused, even indirectly, by abuse?"

"We have no reason to believe that it was. The people at her office called an ambulance Friday afternoon. She had severe cramping and bleeding. I met them here but she lost the baby right away. The bleeding was so severe that I didn't feel it was possible to transport her to a larger hospital. I did all I could for her."

Sally was looking pretty white by this time, and I didn't want to frighten her with any more graphic details. But something about the explanation didn't sit right with me. Santa Fe was only thirty minutes away. Surely an ambulance driving full bore could have gotten her there in time.

I wanted to ask a few more questions, but Rod Phillips' face had closed down. He suddenly had something to do with the files on the desk. He stood and held his hand out, clearly dismissing us.

"Sally. Good to see you again." The friendly brown eyes had cooled. "Charlie. Nice to meet you."

Why did he want to protect an abuser? I knew that doctor-patient confidentiality was practically sacred, but I was also pretty sure that if a doctor knew a crime had been committed, he had to report it. What was going on here? Maybe Rod Phillips was a good friend of Richard Martinez, and was turning his back on the obvious evidence.

Back in the car, I turned to Sally again. Her color was coming back slowly.

"Well," I said, "that didn't get us very far."

"That poor woman." Sally's voice was shaky.

"Hey, don't you worry," I said, patting her hand. "It's not going to happen to you."

I hoped I sounded convincing.

6

We stopped back by Laura Armijo's house, but found no one home. I wrote a quick note on the back of one of my business cards, telling her we'd had no luck, but to call me if I could help. I stuck the card in her mailbox.

It was almost noon, and we had decided there wasn't much else we could accomplish here. We checked out of the motel and hit the road. Traffic between Valle Escondido and Santa Fe wasn't bad. It was still early in the day. I treated Sally to lunch in Santa Fe at one of those trendy touristy places with rip-off prices. The atmosphere was nice, though, and we took our time. By the time we each polished off a slice of cheesecake, she was able to laugh again, although she conveyed a certain anxiety to see her husband and hold onto him.

The temperature in Albuquerque was still over a hundred degrees when we arrived at four o'clock. Even with the air conditioning running full blast, we could feel it. The roadways looked wavy in the heat, and bright white glared off the wind-shields of oncoming cars. Coping with it tired me out.

I dropped Sally at her house in the northeast heights, then headed across town to my place. I live in the old country club section of town, near historic Old Town. It's the house I grew up in. I have the same neighbors, the same lawn, the same trees that I've always known. The homes aren't fabulous by today's stand-ards, but I like the familiarity and comfort of the place. The ride across town took about twenty minutes. By the time I pulled into my own driveway, I was more than ready to hug my dog and kiss the ground.

Since my only baggage consisted of the newly purchased toothbrush and T-shirt, I stuffed them into my purse and walked around the side of the house. Rusty would either be waiting in the backyard or next door at Mrs. Higgins'. I didn't get accosted as I entered the side gate, so I walked through the break in the hedge to my neighbor's back porch. She must have seen me coming, because the door opened and all sixty pounds of Rusty bounded out.

He covered my hands with lovely doggy kisses, then leaned against me so hard I thought we'd both fall over. Rusty is an unusual breed, with the build of a Lab and the color of an Irish Setter. He smiled at me with that special grin of his that makes most people think he's snarling.

"Hi, Charlie, good to see you home." Elsa Higgins waited in the doorway. "Want to come in for a glass of tea?"

I wanted to kick off my shoes and have a shower, but felt a little guilty that I hadn't spent much time with my elderly neigh-bor recently. Especially when I frequently called on her for favors.

Rusty stayed close at my heels as I climbed the two steps to her back door. The kitchen was overly warm, and smelled of vegetable soup. I could see a large pot steaming on the back burner.

"I've got some tea made right here," she said, "and it will just take a minute to put ice in these glasses."

Two glasses waited on the worn counter top. She'd obviously been planning this little social visit. Though she seems to stay busy all the time, I know she loves company. Even a small event like sharing iced tea meant a lot to her. I needed to spend more time with her.

Elsa Higgins, 'Gram' as my brothers and I call her, had lived alone almost as long as I could remember. Now eighty-six, she had been widowed twenty-some years ago. Mr. Higgins was a dim memory for me, a white-haired old man who used to putter in the garden a lot. He'd been long gone by the time I moved in with Gram after my parent's untimely death. She, too, had been gray for as long as I could remember, but age hasn't put much of a damper on her. She's feisty and opinionated, and I want to be just like her when I grow up.

She scooted to the freezer, where she pulled out an old metal ice tray. A couple of cubes flew upward as she wrestled with the ancient thing, trying to loosen the batch.

"Here, let me try that for you," I suggested.

She seemed glad to let me have it. I didn't have a lot better luck at first, but eventually extracted enough cubes for two glasses. Why did she fight this old relic when the new plastic trays were so much easier? Maybe I'd pick up a couple for her on my next trip to the store.

"Why don't we go in the living room?" she asked. "This kitchen's hot with that soup kettle going. I don't know what I was thinking on a hot day like this."

Rusty followed us into the cooler part of the house. Her house is about the same size as mine — three bedrooms, living room, dining, kitchen, two baths. She seems to live in two rooms, the kitchen and living room. I don't know what she does with the rest of the space. It's full of stuff, though, I've seen that much. All her furniture is vintage 1940s, and hasn't changed since my earliest childhood recollections. She even has crocheted antimacassars on all the chairs and sofas.

A large brown rocker is Gram's favorite chair, so I opted for the sofa beside it, setting my iced tea on a coaster on the coffee table.

"Did Rusty behave himself last night?" I asked.

"Oh, sure. He's always a good boy."

The subject of the conversation raised his head, knowing we were talking about him. Elsa gave him a sweet smile, and he thwapped his tail against the floor. When he realized that no treats were forthcoming, he returned to his stretched-out position.

"Thanks for taking care of him on such short notice." I went on to explain how it happened that Sally and I stayed overnight in Valle Escondido.

"We left the whole thing kind of unfinished," I told her. "I'm not sure whether I'm expected to do anything more or not. I mean, no one really asked us to investigate. But then, there's a situation where a woman shouldn't have died, but she did."

"It sounds so sad," she commented.

A minute or two of silence passed.

"So, when does your beau arrive?"

"Thursday night. God, that's only three more days." Somehow the time had crept along for the last month, only to begin racing these last few days.

"Well, you bring him over here to meet me."

"It'll be late Thursday night," I told her. Somehow, after being apart two months, during which our phone conversations had become rather steamy, I didn't think visiting the neighbors would be first on our agenda. "I'll bring him over on Friday."

My iced tea was finished. Although it felt like I was cutting the visit short, I was weary from my travels, and ready to relax on my own soil. Rusty jumped up as soon as I stood.

"C'mon kid, let's get going."

The mailbox was empty. It was a holiday, after all. Rusty and I dined on instant noodles, the kind you pour boiling water over and wait three minutes for. I didn't have the energy for much else. A hot shower and fresh clothes felt good, and afterward I curled up on the couch with a book.

I had a hard time settling in with it, though. Drake would be here in three more days, and I kept noticing disorder around the house that should be cleaned up. Rusty and I rarely do major damage, but even the neatest people have to straighten up now and then. I finally set the book aside and picked up the feather duster. An hour later, the place looked much better. I would change the sheets and run the vacuum cleaner the night before he arrived.

I went to bed around nine, to the sound of distant bottle rockets whizzing through the air.

The sun came through my window early the next morning. After three days off, I was out of the habit of moving at this hour. However, Rusty wasn't. He got up off his rug at the foot of my bed and proceeded to lick my fingers until I stirred. I threw on a robe and let him out the back door, while I headed toward the bathroom.

Fifteen minutes later, I had donned a cotton shirt and pants, pulled my hair into a ponytail, and done my usual minimal makeup routine, consisting of blusher and lipstick. Rusty waited at the back door for breakfast, so I let him in. He had a scoop of nuggets in his bowl, while I poured yogurt over granola for myself.

We were on our way to the office before the traffic got bad. The office Ron and I share is only about a mile or so from home, in an old Victorian house. The neighborhood is in transition from residential to business, and has been that way for years. Except for discreet placards on the sides of some of the places, one would never know it wasn't just a quiet residential area.

Ours is painted pale gray with white trim. A driveway beside the house leads to a parking area in back, beside the original carriage house. Inside, the old parlor serves as a reception area, the dining room for conferences, and the kitchen is . . . what else? Upstairs, the former bedrooms have become Ron's and my offices. There's a bathroom and storage room.

Since I practically live here, I've made my own office as homey as possible, with antiques, hanging plants, and an oriental rug. Ron has his own decor: a desk heaped with files and papers. We limit his decorating freedom to that one room.

Mine was the first vehicle in the parking area. Rusty leaped out as soon as I opened the car door, and proceeded to check the perimeter of the yard. I unlocked the back door, switched on lights, and started the coffee maker. Saturday's mail lay in a heap under the mail slot at the front door. I carried it upstairs with me. Rusty followed, his toenails clicking on the hardwood floors.

The coffee smell reached me, so I went back down, poured a cup, and took it upstairs to drink while I opened the mail. Sally came in a short while later. She peeked her head in my doorway to let me know she'd arrived.

"You look a little green around the edges," I told her. Actually, pale was more like it.

"Yeah," she said, weakly. "It took me half a package of soda crackers to get out of bed this morning."

Ugh. And she'd actually gotten into this condition on purpose. Not for me. No way. No thanks.

"Is something burning, or does the coffee always smell this strong?" she asked.

"No, this is how it always smells."

She looked like she might bolt for the bathroom.

"Sally, would you like to take some time off? I'm sure we could manage."

She took a deep breath, and a little color returned to her face. "No, I need to work. If I stayed home, I'd lie around all day and get fat."

"I hate to tell you this, but I think you're gonna get fat anyway."

That perked her up a little. She chuckled, but her normally infectious smile was wan.

"Seriously, we could rearrange your hours if you want. You could work afternoons instead of mornings."

"Let's see how it goes. This is the first morning I've felt really rotten. If it keeps up, I may take you up on the offer."

She took her mail and headed for her desk. I sorted mine into piles according to urgency. The first week of the month, my most urgent task is usually to make my general ledger entries and get the previous month closed out so we could begin billing the new month. Exciting stuff.

A couple of hours passed with me so engrossed in numbers that I didn't budge from my desk. Somehow I'd gotten one entry inverted, so my cash balance just wasn't coming out right. I finally decided a little break might help. Sometimes numbers look clearer when you can step back from them a bit.

It occurred to me that I hadn't heard from Ron yet, so I peeked into his office. Same clutter, no Ron. Downstairs, Sally was typing a letter. She looked a lot better. A waxed paper tube of saltines lay open beside the typewriter.

"No Ron yet?" I asked.

"Oh, I forgot to tell you. He had an appointment, and said he'd be in about three."

Just as well. Ron and I had had an argument Friday afternoon that was still a little fresh. I had a feeling it might be awkward when we came face to face again. It was an old issue, which had been once again thrust into the limelight at the climax of the last case I'd helped out on. Guns. I don't like them, Ron does.

Standing now in the hallway outside the reception area brought it all back again, a little too close. Less than a month ago, a murderer had gotten the two of us cornered here in the office. It was up to me to get the gun from Ron's desk drawer and use it. And that was the source of our conflict. Ignoring the debate was not making it go away. I knew Ron would bring it up again. This week.

I stomped into the kitchen and splashed more coffee into my cup. This was not how I wanted the week to go. I wanted to be planning a romantic getaway with Drake Langston, not having a fight with my brother over gun control.

7

At three o'clock Ron walked in and placed the gun on my desk. It lay there, a dull black deadly-looking thing. My insides tightened.

"You know how I feel about this, Ron," I warned.

"I know." He stood before me, a middle-aged balding man in faded Levis and plaid shirt. His eyes were sympathetic, but his mouth was firm. "You've got to overcome the fear, Charlie."

That was the hard part. Mainly because I didn't like to acknowledge fear. I like to think of myself as this independent, modern, fearless woman. But, around the gun, it was there. He was right, the word for it was fear.

I'd already given all the arguments about gun control. About how many accidents there are in homes every year involving guns bought for protection of the family. About how many domestic violence scenes turned deadly because of a gun already in the house. And Ron had argued about the stupidity of not being able to protect oneself. About becoming a victim needlessly. About learning to protect myself. And the hell of it was, because of the incident right here in this office, I was having to admit that he was right.

He came around the desk, knelt down, and took my hands.

"Look, hon, I'm only pressing this issue because I love you."

That brought tears to my eyes.

"I'd never forgive myself if something happened to you, and I could've taught you how to protect yourself."

My lower lip quivered a little. I bit down on it to make it stop. It is not like me to break into tears like this.

"Charlie, I'm not going to let us stay mad at each other over this. You know my view and I know yours. The offer is there. I'll take you out to the shooting range and show you the safe way to use the gun. But only when *you* say it's time."

He stood up and holstered the gun. I heard him walk across the hall to his own office.

Damn! I wanted so badly to stay firm and fight for my cause. It was killing me to admit that Ron was right. But what kind of fool was I, knowing that I routinely get myself into dangerous situations, where I might not be able to protect myself? I pulled a Kleenex from the box on my desk and sniffed into it a couple of times.

My legs dragged but I made them do it. I walked across the hall to Ron's doorway.

"It's time." I said.

He looked up and smiled tentatively.

"Just don't give me any of that sanctimonious I-told-you-so shit," I warned him.

"Yes, ma'am." He stood up. "We could go out to the range now," he suggested.

Obviously, he figured that given the chance I would bolt. He was probably right. No time like the present.

"Do I have to dress for this?" I pictured fatigues, belts of bullets strapped across my chest, black and green face paint.

"Nope, you're fine."

Sally had left at noon, and there were no pressing matters that I could dream up. The phones had been deadly quiet all afternoon. The machine could answer for awhile.

With all the enthusiasm I usually reserve for trips to the dentist, I followed Ron out to his car. Rusty hopped into the back seat of the Mustang convertible. He had no trouble getting excited about the trip. Ron put the holstered gun into a tote box he kept in the trunk.

The gun range is way out past the farthest reaches of the very absolute westernmost edge of the city. Way out there. It felt like hours before we arrived. Secluded isn't the word for it. Ron's membership entitled him to carry a key to the gate. He drove through, then got out to reclose it behind us. The late afternoon sun blasted the desert earth. There was no breeze to relieve the heat, nor to stir up the dust.

We parked near a row of wooden tables and benches. A small wooden building stood to one side. Large dirt berms stood in ranks at various distances ahead of us. The closest were probably twenty-five yards away. Ron set the tote box on one of the tables, then led the way to the wooden building. There he unlocked a padlocked door. Inside were all sorts of strange looking parapher-nalia. The only items which looked familiar to me were paper targets with black bullseyes in the middle. He picked up a few of them and led me back outside. I tagged along like a little kid.

Rummaging through the tote box, he came up with a staple gun. We trudged out to the closest row of dirt hills, and Ron began to staple paper targets to frames erected in front of the dirt. I held the paper in place as he stapled, really getting into the spirit of the thing. Once we had four targets in place, we hiked back to the table. Now for the fun part.

"Okay," he began in authoritarian form. "First rule of the range is that you never handle your weapon when anyone else is down range."

I nodded.

"Second rule. Always be aware of where your weapon is pointed. Don't be lollygagging around, staring off every which way, and waving your gun around."

Being a person who is seldom given to lollygagging, I thought I could handle that one.

"Now. Loading the weapon." He pulled the gun from its holster. He slid a full magazine of bullets into the grip. Next he held it out to me, guiding my hands to hold it correctly.

"This is a Beretta 9mm semi-automatic weapon," he said. "That means after you fire your first shot, it's cocked and ready to fire another, and another, until the magazine is empty. You can't forget that. The gun is hot unless you de-cock it." He showed me how.

"Here's how you aim it." He drew a little sketch to show me how to line up the front and back sights.

"Shall I demonstrate?"

I was glad to let him have first shot, although I was beginning to feel a little intrigued by the whole process. From the box he first pulled out two headsets. "Always wear your ears for practice," he said. "Otherwise, you'll be deaf before you know it." We both slipped the "ears" on.

Ron gripped the gun, taking time to show me how to hold it, to avoid being smacked by the slide as it automatically loaded the next bullet. I stood back as he aimed and fired. Fifteen shots in as many seconds.

"You want to shoot now, or shall we check the target first?"

"Let me shoot some, then we can check them both." Careful, Charlie, you'll start sounding enthusiastic.

I took the gun, replaced the empty magazine with a full one, just like Ron showed me, then imitated his stance in aiming at the target. Slowly and carefully I lined up the sights, just like he'd said. Slowly and carefully I pulled the trigger. Four more times.

"Okay," he shouted. "Let's check the target before you fire them all. Until you get used to the gun, you're just wasting bullets unless you know where they're going."

I remembered to de-cock the gun before lowering it.

"Always flip the safety on if you're going to carry the gun around," he said.

I did. I even remembered to point the gun off to the side as we walked down range. Of Ron's fifteen shots, twelve were in the black area of the target.

"Wow," he said, "I'm sure out of practice."

Of my five shots, two were in the white outer area. The other three were nowhere to be seen. I couldn't believe it. I'd aimed so carefully.

"See why you don't want to own a gun if you never practice with it?" he said.

I was beginning to see that maybe both the gun control people and gun advocates had their points.

"What happened? I was so careful in my aiming."

"It just takes a lot of practice, and being thoroughly familiar with your own weapon. They're all different. Come on, we'll mark these shots, and you can do some more."

He gave me a couple of pointers, and I fired five more shots. This time all five were on the target, one in the black area. All fifteen of Ron's shots went into the black this time. Four of them were in the smallest inner circle. On the next round, Ron allowed me to move in a little closer to the targets.

"If you were shooting an intruder in the house, he wouldn't be twenty-five yards away. Practice awhile at about fifteen yards."

My improvement was immediate. I fired fifteen shots, ten of which were in the black. I was actually beginning to enjoy this. We took turns, firing from the fifteen yard mark part of the time, and from twenty-five yards at other times. By the end of two hours, I was getting all my shots on the target. My success with the bullseye was sporadic. My arms were beginning to tremble from the strain.

"What do you think?" Ron asked, as we packed away the stuff. "Kind of fun, huh?"

I have a difficult time admitting a change in attitude, but I think he knew. He was cool enough about it not to say I-told-you-so.

"We can come out again, anytime you want," he said. "I try to get out here two or three times a week."

I told him to count me in. By the time he dropped me back at the office where I'd left my Jeep parked, the sun was low in the sky. I felt tired and dusty, but I was also starving.

"How about enchiladas at Pedro's?" I invited.

No one who's ever had them can turn down enchiladas at Pedro's. He decided to follow me there.

Pedro's missed being a tourist attraction by about a block. Just off the main plaza in Old Town, most visitors pass it by in favor of the expensive places. It's a small adobe building, with living quarters at the back where Pedro and his wife Concha settled after their kids all grew up. The two of them take turns cooking, tending bar, and waiting tables. They make the best margarita in town, and enchiladas that non-New Mexicans can't even imagine.

Two of the five parking spaces out front were taken. Ron and I filled two more. I recognized one of the vehicles as a dusty pickup truck belonging to Manny, a regular here. The other also looked local, so I figured it was safe to take Rusty in. Pedro saves me a corner table, where Rusty enjoys his own shadowy spot and waits for tortilla chips to fall his way. As long as the place isn't crowded, which is rare, Pedro doesn't worry about this little violation of the health code.

Inside, a large Mexican carved wooden bar fills the entire back wall. There are half a dozen tables. Manny sat at his regular spot, which is across the room from my regular spot. He raised his shot glass to us as we entered. He wears beaten down jeans with thick brown boots, either a striped or plaid shirt (tonight it was the stripe), and a straw hat that looks like it's been stomped on by more than a few horses. His leathery brown face always has about three days growth of black and white speckled beard. His dusty fingers are usually wrapped around a shot glass of tequila. He wins his drinks by betting with gringos on how hot he can take his chile. Pedro claims Manny has the insides of a teenager.

Rusty went straight to his corner, while Ron and I took seats across from each other. Pedro had smiled his big white smile as we came in. He was occupied with taking an order from those at the other table, but still managed to get our drink order by raising two fingers toward us then pointing at the bar. I nodded. Two minutes later, we each had a glass of foaming margarita with salt crystals thick on the rim.

"So! When does that special man get here?" Concha caught me in mid-sip. She beamed down at me like the mother of the bride. She tends to move my relationships along faster than I do.

"Day after tomorrow," I answered.

"Well, you bring him here first thing," she instructed. "Papa and I gotta approve this guy, you know."

I hoped Drake was ready for this. Having been an independent soul all his life, I wasn't sure how he'd take to being adopted by the local restaurateurs. Well, he'd have to learn.

Meanwhile, Pedro appeared with two steaming plates of chicken enchiladas, smothered in green chile sauce and topped with sour cream.

"So, what did you and Sally end up doing on your drive north?" Ron asked.

I told him about our visit to Laura Armijo and about the death of her friend, Cynthia. How Sally had wanted to stay over and find out what happened.

"It seemed strange to me, Ron, how the doctor didn't seem the least bit concerned about whether Cynthia's husband had caused the miscarriage. He tried to make light of it, but he was keeping something from us."

"Well, even if he knew or suspected abuse he can't discuss that with everyone who asks. Doctor/patient confidentiality, remember? After all, you aren't a law officer. You didn't even know this woman."

Guess that put me in my place. He was correct, but that didn't make it right. If Richard had beaten Cynthia, shouldn't he be held accountable?

We finished our enchiladas, slurped the last of the salt off the margarita glasses, and chatted a few more minutes with Pedro and Concha before leaving. Somehow, though, I couldn't forget Cynthia's face.

8

"The abuser will almost always be contrite afterward. He'll plead forgiveness, he'll promise it won't happen again, he may even cry as he's making these promises."

I looked around at the women in the room. Several heads were nodding.

"Or he'll try to make it seem like your fault. He had to hit you because you were bad or stupid."

More heads nodded.

I'd looked up the battered women's shelter in the phone book, and decided to attend a group counseling session without letting on what I was up to. The speaker was a woman of about thirty-five or so, dressed casually in a cotton batik print skirt and loose fitting cotton sweater. Her blond hair framed her face with permed curls. Her slim hands worked as she talked, as though trying to paint a better picture for those she spoke to.

The ten women in the room were various ages, shapes, and backgrounds. Some had small children with them. The kids had been encouraged to play in another room at the beginning of the session.

"The thing you have to remember," she continued, emphasizing each word, "is that even if you do a stupid thing, it doesn't give anyone the right to hit you. The abuser is the one who's wrong, not the victim."

"But why does he do this to me?" The questioner was a young woman, no more than twenty, with a purple bruise next to her left eye.

"Because he's got problems," the speaker told her. "Problems that started long before you came into the picture. He continues this behavior because he gets away with it."

"But I've tried fighting back," another woman said. She was in her fifties, the kind of woman who should have been sitting on the front porch with a grandchild on her lap. "He just gets more violent. I've tried leaving, but he threatens, or worse yet, he'll cry."

The questions became more emotional, but the answers were always sensible and calm. I couldn't imagine staying with someone who treated me the way these women described. But then, I hadn't been faced with that decision. In college I'd been engaged once. His name was Brad North, and two weeks before the wedding he'd eloped with my best friend, Stacy. I run into Stacy every now and then. She and Brad live in the most upscale part of town; she drives a Mercedes, has gorgeous clothes and lots of jewelry. But something in her face always remains tight, hidden. Much like some of the looks I was seeing here today. I don't know what secrets she hides, but I'm thankful to have narrowly escaped that trap.

My mind wandered away from the questions and answers. I found myself watching the women's faces, their emotions, for clues about Cynthia. What little characteristics could I ask Laura about? Cynthia must have dropped hints as to what was going on.

I thought of the way Richard had looked that night, his haggard face, his tangled hair, his red rimmed eyes.

The session was over, and the women gathered at the back of the room for coffee and donuts. I slipped out the back door. I thought I had heard enough for now.

Outside, the air was still and hot enough to bake cookies. The sky was a deep solid blue. No sign of a rain cloud. Cicadas scratched out their rhythmic, tiresome noise. It was the fourth day in a row of hundred degree temperatures, and I was ready for a break. By the time we got any storms everything would be just dry enough to make top grade fuel for the lightning. I thought again of the forests around Valle Escondido.

At the office, Sally had left a note on my desk. Laura Armijo had called. According to Sally's comment on the note, "She said it wasn't urgent, but I get the feeling it is." I dialed the number, but there was no answer.

Ron's note said he would be at the County Courthouse researching public records all afternoon. There were no appointments scheduled; I had my own work fairly well caught up, so I decided to switch on the answering machine and go home.

Rusty was glad to see me. Usually he goes to the office with me, but today, knowing that I'd be at that meeting quite awhile, I'd left him home. He raced around the backyard several times to express his joy, then flopped on the floor at my feet while I flipped through the mail. Drake had sent a copy of his itinerary so I'd know what time to pick him up at the airport. Tomorrow already. I hoped his time here wouldn't fly by as quickly as these last few days had.

I put on shorts and a T-shirt, thinking I'd vacuum and tidy up the house one more time. It was too hot to work, though. I talked myself into having a glass of lemonade instead and waiting until after dark to vacuum. I watched half of a talk show on TV, but got restless . The subject was so outlandishly stupid I couldn't believe the people on the screen were taking it seriously.

Laura Armijo still didn't answer when I tried her number a second time, so I stuck the note in my purse for tomorrow and made myself a salad for dinner. It was nine o'clock before the house cooled off enough to be cleaned. It took me about an hour to give it the once-over, then I took a shower and went to bed, still wondering what Laura would have called about.

I woke up early. The room was light, but the sun had not yet peeked over the top of Sandia Crest. Drake would be here tonight. My stomach tightened with anticipation. I had already warned Ron and Sally that I didn't plan to be in the office much over the next few days. Today would be my chance to get my desk cleared so I could have guilt-free time off.

The light on the answering machine was blinking frantically when I arrived at the office. The only call was from Laura. It had come in at seven forty-five. She said she would be leaving for work soon, but I could give her a call there. She left two numbers, her home and the bank.

No one answered at the home number so I dialed the bank.

"Oh, Charlie, I'm glad you called." Laura sounded genuinely relieved to hear my voice.

"Is there a problem?"

"I attended Cynthia's funeral yesterday," she said. "It was so sad. There's something I thought you should know," her voice dropped to a bare whisper, "but I really can't talk about it here. Is there any chance you could come back up this weekend?"

With Drake arriving tonight I didn't want to commit my time to anyone else.

"I don't know, Laura. Isn't it something you can tell me over the phone? I could call you back."

Her voice was barely audible now. Obviously someone else was nearby. "The police are involved now, Charlie," she whispered. "And I'm getting scared."

The phone clicked, and it took me a minute to realize I was hanging onto a dead instrument. What was that all about? I returned the receiver to its cradle slowly. Laura obviously was scared, but of what? Or whom? It wouldn't do me any good to call her back at work. I'd try her home again around dinner time tonight. Maybe she'd open up then.

The stack of papers in my "IN" basket was dwindling satisfactorily when Ron stuck his head in my doorway. He wore a sports jacket and tie causing me to do a double take.

"What're you so dressed up for?" This was a real departure from his usual western shirt and Levi's.

"Court. I have to testify in the Perkins case."

I felt my lip wrinkle up. "Ugh, not fun," I said. Last year, Ron had been hired by friends to do a background check on a woman. Bill Perkins was a successful businessman, divorced from wife number one less than a year. He'd been swept off his feet by a vivacious younger woman, Jennifer. Supplied with suspicions from Bill Perkins' friends, Ron had traced Jennifer's background and found quite a few unsavory tidbits, including two former marriages and several brushes with the law. Unfortunately, Perkins hadn't listened to the evidence before the wedding. Now, six months later, he was paying the price. The new Mrs. Perkins had transferred many of his assets to her name, had drained several of his bank accounts, and was already flaunting a new man. But Bill couldn't get rid of her. She liked the lifestyle and refused to budge.

The irony of this whole thing is that Ron was still recovering from a disastrous fling with a younger woman himself. Maybe that's why he took Bill Perkins' case to heart.

"You gonna be here all day?" he asked me now.

"I'm not sure. Once I get the payables out of the way, and last week's billing done, I should be through here. I wasn't planning to stay late." Drake's flight would arrive at eight, and I found myself planning the day in reverse, allowing time for everything I wanted to get done. I didn't want to show up at the airport late and flustered.

Ron grinned. He had known, ever since he picked me up at the airport when I arrived home from Hawaii, that I'd met someone special. His own quick fling had occupied his mind at the time, but at least he wasn't one to begrudge me, just because his affair hadn't worked out.

"Don't plan on seeing me around here tomorrow, though," I added with a grin of my own.

"You will bring him by here to meet us, won't you?"

"Sometime."

"Charlie?" Ron's face had become serious all of a sudden. He stood in my doorway, shifting from one foot to the other. "You won't let yourself do anything stupid, will you?" I knew he was thinking of Vicky, his recent love disaster.

"I'll sure try not to." How can one promise what will happen in matters of the heart? No matter how well prepared we think we are, some things seem to run out of control. It had been more than two years since I'd had any kind of romantic relationship, and maybe I was overdue. I'd told myself that I'd be careful when I first met Drake Langston. Now, after being apart for close to two months, I hoped I could keep that promise.

Sally buzzed me on the intercom to tell me she was going home for the day, and I realized with a start that it was already noon. I had barely acknowledged her arrival this morning.

"Laura Armijo didn't call back, by chance?" I asked.

"No . . . Why?" I guess I had forgotten to tell Sally about my call to Laura. I briefly relayed the gist of this morning's conversation. Sally knew nothing about any update of the events in Valle Escondido.

"Do you want me to call her for you?" she asked.

"No, I got the feeling she couldn't talk at work. I think I'll call her again this evening."

With that, Sally said she'd go on home. We wished each other a good weekend. At some point an hour or so later, Ron left for court giving me a quick wave as he left. I stayed with my paperwork until it was done, and was pleased to see that it was still only three o'clock. Not feeling too guilty, I gathered my briefcase and my dog and locked up the place.

With my eyes frequently on the clock, the rest of the afternoon dragged. Finally, it was seven, a justifiable time to leave for the airport.

9

The terminal was jammed with people, everyone in a hurry to get somewhere. Noise rebounded off the tile floors. The paging system droned constantly, voices almost overlapping each other. It had taken me close to fifteen minutes just to find a parking space in the crowded garage. I arrived at the gate just as the plane rolled to a stop. Faces were invisible behind the tiny airplane windows, and I wondered if one of them was Drake. Perhaps he could see me silhouetted in the large window of the terminal.

Waiting off to one side as the passengers disembarked, I went through all sorts of scenarios. What if I forgot what he looked like? What if he forgot what I looked like? What if he walked right past me? What if I'd forgotten to put on deodorant? Oh, God.

Finally, behind a wide woman laden with three carry-on bags, I thought I spotted his dark hair. Our eyes met at the same moment. He was even handsomer than I remembered. He pushed toward me with open arms. The long embrace felt so familiar that all the "what ifs" disappeared. The smell of him, the feel of my cheek against his shoulder, his strong hands on my back, all took me back to the ten days we'd spent together.

We stood at arm's length finally. His brown eyes looked a little damp around the edges. The dark hair with touches of gray at the temples, the wide smile that had first caught my attention, the sureness in his stance—this was the same Drake that I remembered.

"Oh, Charlie, I missed you," he said. There was a slight quiver in his voice, and both his hands had mine encased in a tight hold.

Unmindful of the jostling crowd around us and the constant noise of the airport paging system, we stood there, a little island of our own. I had missed him, too. More than I knew.

"What do you want to do first?" I asked, as we gradually joined the moving throng of people heading toward the baggage claim.

He grinned lecherously. Stupid question. We'd talked of nothing else in our last conversation.

"I meant, are you hungry? Did they give you dinner on the plane? Would you like to eat something on the way, or would you rather settle in first?"

"Yes, no, no, yes," he said.

I forgot that I tend to ask questions in bunches.

His suitcase was a long time in coming off the line, and we waited at the side, holding hands, not saying a lot. I don't think he took his eyes off me once. Somehow we got through the baggage claim, the airport garage, and the freeway traffic. I tried to concentrate on my driving, but truthfully, I don't remember much about the trip. The night air was warm and we drove with the windows down. He gazed around at the city lights, absorbing the surroundings.

"Our air probably feels awfully dry to you," I said.

"Not bad," he answered. "I grew up in the southwest, remember?"

That's right. He had told me. Arizona, mostly. His family had moved around quite a bit, but his parents were settled now in Flagstaff. Of his ten day vacation he planned to spend a week with me, then drop in on them for the remaining three days on his way back to Hawaii. I decided not to think about the leaving yet.

"Albuquerque sure has changed," he commented. He had been stationed here for about a year during his days in the military. But that was twenty years ago. Since then, the city had sprawled in every direction.

I pointed out a few of the newer landmarks. The downtown skyline, which had grown a little more impressive in recent years with the mayor's push toward renovation, and the general spread of new businesses everywhere. We had joined the westward flow on I-40 now, and were about to exit at Rio Grande Blvd.

"I sure don't remember all the graffiti," he said.

"Gangs. I guess they're getting to be a problem everywhere," I answered. "My neighborhood is a quiet little enclave in the midst of a pretty rough area." I didn't want to tell him that a mere six blocks from my house is an area where most people feel a little shaky driving during the day. Anyone sensible doesn't venture there at all at night.

I caught his look of concern. "Don't worry, Drake. I grew up here. I know the place and I'm used to it." I gave his hand what I hoped was a reassuring squeeze.

My own winding street was quiet and peaceful. Most of the residents of this neighborhood are old enough to be my grandparents and they settle in pretty early. Many of the houses were already dark. Old fashioned street lamps cast yellow circles of light periodically across the sidewalks, illuminating neat lawns and shrubs. The yard service had been to my house the day before. I hoped Drake would be pleased with his first impression of the place.

He was looking at me, not the yard, I noticed when I switched off the ignition. I leaned over to sample his wonderful mouth once more. Suddenly we both wanted to go inside. Drake grabbed his suitcase from the back seat while I unlocked the front door. I'd left lamps on, dim ones that made the living room feel cozy with its oriental rugs, hardwood floors, antique tables, and overstuffed sofa and chairs. Rusty met us at the door.

"Look, he's smiling!" Drake recognized Rusty's silly grin right away.

Rusty edged toward Drake's outstretched hand with a coyness I haven't seen in him before. He rubbed his side against Drake's legs, while Drake obliged him with a good rough back scratch. I needn't have worried about whether Drake would get along with my dog.

After a minute of this affectionate exploitation, Rusty bounded out of the room.

"He's going to bring you an old scummy tennis ball," I said. "He'll expect you to throw it across the room for him, whereupon he'll bring it right back and want a repeat performance until you're sick of the game."

Drake was a good sport, throwing the ball three times before I inserted myself between the two of them. "Enough already," I told Rusty. He dropped the ball and flopped down on the floor.

"Are you hungry?" I asked Drake, starting toward the kitchen.

"Yes," he said. He grabbed my hand and spun me around. His kiss was urgent and I found myself returning it equally, and somehow we were in the bedroom.

An hour later I stretched beside him, my head on his shoulder, my fingers playing with the thick hair on his chest.

"Maybe I should rephrase the question," I said. "Would you like food?"

He laughed and rolled toward me. "Yeah, I think I worked up a little appetite."

I found a light cotton robe to put on. Drake had left his suitcase in the living room. He strolled out naked to get it. Rusty looked at me with questioning eyes. He wasn't used to being locked out of the bedroom.

"Sorry, old boy," I said, "that's life."

I rummaged around in the refrigerator and came up with cheese, crackers, fruit, and a bottle of wine. By the time Drake emerged from the shower, warm and damp, with his dark hair curling slightly above his ears, I had arranged a presentable tray of snacks.

"Kitchen, living room, or bedroom?" I asked.

He thought for a minute. "Living room," he said. "If I get you back in that bedroom, I doubt if I'll be thinking about food."

Big talker.

We set the food tray on the coffee table and I lit a couple of candles.

"I like this house," he said, looking around the room, then at me. "It's you."

"What do you mean?"

"Neat, organized, warm, lovely . . ." His eyes glowed with appreciation.

"Oh, please, I'm just me. Same person you met in Hawaii, same person who dashes off getting into trouble all the time."

"What kind of trouble are you in now?" he asked. The dark brows pulled together a little in front.

"Well, I'm not. Not exactly. A friend of Sally's is, sort of." I don't think I was explaining it too well. I told him a little about the situation in Valle Escondido.

"Would you be interested in driving up there over the weekend?" I asked.

"Sure. I don't remember too much about northern New Mexico," he said, "except there are some really pretty mountains."

"Then you'll like Valle Escondido. It's beautiful country up there."

He took my hand and raised my fingers to his lips. "I love you, Charlie," he said. His voice was husky.

The words took me by surprise. His dark eyes held mine for a very long minute. An emotion long buried surfaced. "I love you too, Drake." I was pretty sure I meant it.

10

The room was dark. A strong arm encircled my waist. Something rough scratched at my bare shoulder. I came awake with a start. Drake. Sleeping with another person would take some getting used to. He moaned softly in his sleep and pulled me closer. Our bare legs entwined, and I could feel the hair on his chest against my back. His warmth was comforting; his even breathing lulled me back into the almost narcotic sleep from which I'd come.

The next thing I knew pale gray light filtered through the bedroom window. Drake's side of the bed was empty. I heard a small sound from behind the bathroom door. He emerged, still naked.

"Drake? You okay?"

"Um hmm," he said, sliding between the sheets. "I don't know why I woke up so early."

He reached for me at the same time I reached for him. We made love again until the sun was fully up, then dropped off to sleep. It was after ten when I again became fully conscious. Drake lay curled up on his side, breathing softly. I decided not to disturb him yet.

I took a quick shower and put on shorts and a cotton T-shirt. Rusty waited outside the bedroom door, still puzzled with the new arrangement. He looked anxious to avail himself of the backyard facilities.

After letting him out, I checked the refrigerator for breakfast fixings. Managed to find orange juice, eggs, bread, and a variety of fresh vegetables. I diced the veggies, whipped four eggs in a bowl, and shook the juice so it was foamy on top. I set the breakfast table with my mother's dishes — the ones with the tiny wildflowers on them, and set an omelet pan out, ready to preheat at a moment's notice.

When I walked out front to get the newspaper, I could hear the shower running. I stuck my head in the bedroom. Drake had made the bed neatly and set his suitcase in the corner. His voice came from the shower, humming an Elvis Presley love song. A warm feeling welled up inside me.

Back in the kitchen, I turned on the burner under the omelet pan, poured juice in two glasses, and let Rusty back in. He headed straight for his bowl.

"I like this picture." Drake stood in the doorway, his eyes surveying the kitchen. Dressed in crisp khakis and a polo shirt with helicopter logo on the chest, his trim body was enormously appealing. He came toward me and raised one hand to stroke the side of my face.

"How about a vegetable omelet?"

"Sounds great. How can I help?"

I suggested that he butter the bread and man the toaster oven. Meanwhile I hoped I would remember the knack of turning an omelet without shredding it.

"Well," I said, once we were well into the food, "are you ready to meet the curious hordes?"

He laughed, reminding me once again that his easy-going manner and sense of humor were two of his many attractive qualities.

"Everyone I know is anxious to find out about the man I've been so ga-ga over."

"I think I can handle it," he replied. "Are you ga-ga?"

"More than I thought I'd ever allow myself to be."

He squeezed my hand, then stood up. "I'm doing the dishes," he informed me. "Sink or dishwasher?"

"Dishwasher is fine. If there's not a full load, we'll run them later."

"Meanwhile, you sit here and have another cup of coffee," he said, pouring. "You might need your strength for later." He added this last remark with a wiggle of the eyebrows.

Sitting at the kitchen table, having a second cup of coffee and watching a man wash the dishes was a new experience for me. I felt like I should jump up and do something. But truthfully, it was nice. This, and the fantastic sex had left me feeling euphoric.

Rusty had plopped himself down in the corner, content with the arrangement too. Drake loaded the dishes in record time, and even wiped off the counter tops and stove. This one might just be a keeper.

A soft tapping at the back door interrupted my thoughts. Elsa Higgins' fluff of white hair showed through the windowed panel.

"I saw your shade was raised," she said timidly.

Raising the kitchen window shade has been our signal to each other for years. As she gets older I watch hers especially carefully. Without unnecessarily intruding upon each other's lives, we at least know the other is alive and well every day.

"Come in, come in," I said, stepping back. "Of course, you have to meet Drake."

She beamed at him like she was welcoming a new grandson to the family.

"Well, Drake, I'm so glad to meet you. Charlie's told me all about you."

I caught his look with the widened eyes, and answered with a "well, not *everything*" kind of glance.

"We just finished eating," I told her. "Can I get you a cup of tea?"

Her glance took in the clean kitchen and Drake with dish towel in hand.

"Well, if it's not too much trouble," she said.

"The water's already hot," I assured her. I busied myself with getting tea bag and cup, while Drake folded the dish towel then took a seat at the table beside her.

"I've always wondered what it would be like to ride in a helicopter," she said.

The two of them eased right into a conversation while I acted busy and listened shamelessly. Drake told her about himself, but didn't dominate the conversation. He asked her about herself and about Albuquerque, and even said yes ma'am and no ma'am. I was impressed.

By the time she left about an hour later, I was holding in my laughter.

"Was that a case of major sucking up, or were you really that interested in her stories?" I had to ask.

"Sorry," he said, "I guess I was just raised to be extra polite. Did I overdo it?"

"Not a bit," I said, wrapping my arms around his neck. "You were perfect."

We decided to take a drive, with one stop at the office so Sally and Ron could meet the guest of honor.

The day was hot and still. Leaves on the trees hung tired and dusty, with no hint of wind to stir them. The air smelled like cooked flowers. I turned on the air conditioning in the Jeep and rolled all the windows down for the first few minutes to blow out the hot unbreathable air.

We took our time, cruising the plaza at Old Town. The old church of San Felipe de Neri held the position of honor on one side of the plaza, with adobe shops and restaurants lining the other three sides. A white wooden bandstand sat in the center of the square, deserted now except for groups of tourists strolling and gawking. I told Drake we could come back another afternoon if he wanted to. We drove past Pedro's, one block off the plaza. Enchiladas would be a must during the visit. I couldn't allow a man in my life who wasn't fond of enchiladas.

A few minutes later we were pulling into the parking area at our office. Ron's Mustang sat back there, but Sally's car was gone. I'd forgotten that she would have gone home by now.

Any worries I'd had about how Ron and Drake might get along were quickly set aside. The minute Drake spotted Ron's gun lying on the desk, they found a subject in common.

"A Beretta nine millimeter!"

Ron released the magazine, then opened the slide to drop out the chambered round before handing the gun over.

"Yeah, it's a nice weapon," he said.

Drake handled the gun with respect, keeping it pointed toward the corner of the room, holding it so he could look down the sights.

"This is a beauty," he said, his voice quiet with awe. "I really miss shooting."

"You done much?" Ron asked.

"I used to," Drake said. "But there are no shooting ranges where I live. No chance to go out and do any target practice."

Ron gave him a sympathetic look, as if Drake had told him they didn't allow sex there. Obviously there was something about this brotherhood of target shooters that I had no clue about. They continued a conversation that was about one quarter English and three-quarters some secret man-language.

I wandered across the hall to my own office to see what mail had shown up since yesterday. Not much. Two phone messages

— one from Laura Armijo. Sally had scribbled a note of her own at the bottom, "See me about this first."

Drake and Ron were obviously not missing my company, so I dialed Sally's home number.

"What's up with Laura?" I asked.

She sounded a little groggy. I'd probably awakened her from a nap.

"Laura . . . Laura, let me think."

"The message just gives her phone number, but you wrote that I should see you first," I prompted.

"Oh, yeah." She grunted, like she was struggling to sit up and remember something at the same time. "She wondered if you were coming up there this weekend. Said her last call to you got interrupted."

I remembered that I'd never called Laura back yesterday. Truthfully, I'd kind of let the whole matter slip my mind.

"I'll see if Drake wants to drive up there," I said. "We could make it a little jaunt to get out of the heat here."

"How's the visit going?" Her interest suddenly quickened. "I wanted to be there to meet him."

"He and Ron are in there talking guns right now. I think they've found some kind of blood-brotherhood, or something."

"I meant with you, silly. Is that spark still there?" Her voice came through as mischievous.

Blushing, I assured her that it was. We ended the conversation with me promising that I'd bring Drake back to the office Monday so she could get a chance at him. The other message could wait, so I went back across the hall.

"So, what do you kids have planned for the rest of the week?" Ron asked.

I told him about the need to go up to Valle Escondido for the weekend.

"Drake and I were just talking about getting in some target practice," he said. "Want to plan on the three of us?"

It wasn't exactly how I'd envisioned the week going, but I didn't want to look like the party pooper.

"Sure," I said. "This afternoon? Then we could indulge at Pedro's afterward."

Ron had an errand to do first, so we agreed to meet at the range at five o'clock.

All in all, I didn't embarrass myself too badly at the shooting range. Ron had been right, though, it was a sport that took lots of practice. Drake did a respectable job, considering that he was using someone else's gun and that he hadn't shot at all for several years. All three of us saw some improvement after a couple of hours practice. I had to admit that I enjoyed the challenge, and I noticed a new look of respect toward me in Drake's eyes. There's something about sharing a man's sport with him that forms a bond different than that forged by love alone.

We arrived at Pedro's, hot and dusty and ready for margaritas. Our host, dressed in his customary white pants, shirt, and apron, managed to indulge that desire before Concha emerged from the kitchen to fuss over Drake. Within minutes she had succumbed to his warmth and perhaps just a little to his good looks. I could have sworn she was actually flirting.

"What do you think?" I asked, after he had tasted the enchiladas.

"Umm . . ." He licked his lips and rolled his eyes upward. "I have really missed having good Mexican food. These are the best."

I squeezed his hand, glad that he shared my taste in cuisine. We scraped our plates clean and polished off every bit of margarita. Ron and Drake discovered that they'd both served in the Navy. Ron, naturally, was jealous that Drake had gotten the chance to fly. Helicopter talk and Navy slang dominated the conversation. The two most important men in my life had hit it off.

11

Saturday mornings are meant for lying in bed, snuggled in the warmth of one's lover, arising late, and breakfasting indulgently. We weren't so lucky.

The phone rang at seven. Laura's voice at the other end of the line didn't surprise me. It didn't make me especially happy, either.

"Charlie! Finally, I've caught you at home," she exclaimed almost breathlessly.

I mumbled something impolite, but she didn't seem to notice.

"Are you planning to come up here today?"

Sometime earlier in the week I guess I had left her with that impression. But somehow it irritated me that she would call at seven o'clock to remind me.

"I guess so," I said. "What's up?"

"I've learned about someone else who might have had it in for Cynthia."

"In what way?"

Other voices intruded into the background, and Laura muffled the phone to speak to someone else.

"Sorry, Charlie, I've got company and I need to go. Come by my house when you get here?"

"Okay," I agreed. What was she being so mysterious for?

All hope of sleep was gone now. The phone had awakened Drake, too, and he had proceeded to trail kisses across my shoulder and breasts while I tried to speak coherently with Laura. Since we were awake anyway, we used the time pleasurably.

By nine o'clock we were on the road. The Jeep's gas tank was full, Rusty curled up on the back seat, me driving, Drake sightseeing. We had packed a small overnight bag this time, just in case.

The day was clear and already getting hot. Santa Fe's altitude of seven thousand feet made it somewhat cooler, and I hoped Valle Escondido would be even nicer, tucked up in the mountains as it was.

"I'd forgotten what absolutely clear blue sky looked like," Drake commented. "People think of Hawaii as a sunny tropical paradise, but the fact is we have clouds all the time. I really get sick of battling the rain on my flights."

"Maybe you should be the one thinking about relocating." Even as I said it, I wondered what I was suggesting.

He stared out the window, taking in the rolling hills dotted with piñon. In the distance, Santa Fe Baldy mountain rose, dark green at the bottom, bare above timberline. Thirty minutes later we reached the outskirts of Valle Escondido.

Had it really been seven days since I'd visited here? The little town looked no different. I'd almost swear the same cars sat in the parking lot at Rosa's Cantina. We drew stares from more than one person along the narrow main street. I remembered the winding dirt lane leading to Laura's house and followed it. The sameness here was reassuring. Whatever had frightened Laura enough to call me back here had not changed her neat flowerbeds or the meticulously kept courtyard. Rusty waited in the Jeep, parked in the heavy shade of the old cottonwood, with all the windows down. Drake and I approached the glass paneled door. Laura answered moments after my knock.

"Oh, Charlie, thank God," she breathed. "Come in."

I introduced Drake, and we followed Laura into the cool shadowy living room. She wore a wrinkled white pair of slacks and a striped black and white cotton shirt. Her short dark hair was neat but she wore no makeup. I got the impression that she had dressed hastily. She indicated a leather sofa and we sat, but Laura couldn't seem to hold still. She paced, twisting her fingers together as she spoke.

"The police were here again this morning," she said. "I wasn't sure what to tell them. I just don't know what's going on."

Well, I sure as hell didn't know what was going on, and I was beginning to lose patience with her dramatics. I forced my voice to be calm as I spoke.

"Why don't you start at the beginning, and tell me everything that has happened since Sally and I were here?"

The hand wringing escalated. She had to be in pain.

"Laura, why don't you take a couple of deep breaths, and sit down?" Drake suggested.

She did. Her voice was much steadier when she spoke again.

"The police have been here. Steve Bradley, our police chief, was here this morning asking questions about Richard."

"But that's not why you called me on Thursday," I interjected logically.

"Well, yes and no. I'd heard the police were getting involved."

"What prompted this investigation?" Drake leaned back into the sofa, completely at ease, but obviously curious.

"That's what I called about on Thursday," Laura explained. "Cynthia's funeral Tuesday was . . . well, it was weird."

She rubbed her temples, her eyes closed. "Father Montano had just finished the mass, when Richard stood up and said he wanted to say something. He went to the front of the church and went into this long speech."

Her dark eyes were moist now and her voice had become shaky. I asked whether she would like a glass of water but she refused.

"At first we all thought Richard's talk was going to be a eulogy, that he'd say something about Cynthia or the baby. But he went into this long explanation of his own behavior. Really, most of it didn't even make sense. Several times he got very emotional. He'd cry these great big sobs, then sniff and keep going with his talk. He went on and on until Father led him back to his seat."

"That does sound weird," I said.

"I was sitting with some of the girls from the bank, and Bobby had gone with me. We all left there feeling pretty shaken up."

I thought back to the battered women's group I'd attended. The speaker had said that abusers had a very deep seated need to justify their behavior. Was that what this was all about?

"And you think the police heard about the incident and decided to investigate Richard after all?" I asked.

"No, I think that came because of the fight," she said. She was pacing again.

"Fight?"

"At the cemetery."

"Laura, maybe you better breathe again, sit down, and tell us the rest of it," I suggested.

Drake offered to get some coffee, and she told him where to find the cups. I leaned forward, elbows on knees, to hear what she would come up with next.

"At the cemetery, Richard got into it with Barbara Lewis. Barbara is the bank manager, and Cynthia's immediate supervisor."

"What was their problem?" I asked. Drake came back into the room with three mugs on a small tray. He had found the sugar and creamer, too. I had to admire his resourcefulness.

"Barbara's known among those at the bank as the office witch. She's a tough manager and can be a real bitch at times. Cynthia worked directly under her, and I'm sure Cynthia didn't have it easy. She probably complained to Richard about work sometimes. I mean, everyone does. What are spouses for?"

She calmed visibly as she sipped the coffee. "Anyway, Richard really tied into Barbara, right there in front of the grave. He accused Barbara of killing Cynthia."

12

"Surely he didn't mean that literally?" I could almost feel my mouth hanging open.

"I don't know. He sure sounded like he did."

"What happened next?" Drake asked.

"Barbara defended herself. I mean, she's not one to keep her mouth shut. They got into a real screaming match. Everyone else was really upset by then. Cynthia's mother fainted. Two of his brothers hustled Richard out of there. By the time Mrs. Lovato came to, he was gone, but she still had to be carried to her car. The rest of the crowd was pretty shaken up. We didn't even go to the house afterward."

Again, she looked like she might cry.

"What kinds of questions were the police asking?"

"Mostly about the fight at the cemetery. Someone must have told Steve Bradley about it. That wouldn't be unusual. In a town this size, everyone knows everything about everybody. He wanted to know about Barbara and Cynthia's relationship at work. Had I ever heard Barbara make any threats, that kind of thing."

"Had you?"

"Barbara uses threats as a way of business," she said. "It's a . . . heavy atmosphere at work. We're all afraid of making mistakes. But a death threat? Hardly."

"Did Cynthia take the job threats seriously?" I asked.

"I don't think so," she replied. "All she thought about was the baby. I'm pretty sure she planned to quit work anyway after the baby came. She wanted to be a full-time mother."

Drake and I left a few minutes later. Rusty hung his head out the window as we approached the Jeep, making me feel guilty for leaving him there so long. However, once we got in, I realized it wasn't that hot with all the windows down and the big shady cottonwood tree overhead.

"I think I ought to talk to that police chief," I told Drake. "And maybe the bank manager if we can find her on a weekend. But I feel like this isn't quite how you planned on spending your vacation."

He smiled that beautiful warm smile at me. "Don't worry about me," he said. "I like watching you in action."

I remembered where the police station was from my previous visit. We pulled into the gravel parking lot. The only other car there was a patrol cruiser, a dark blue four-wheel drive with blue and red lights on top. A gold shield-shaped emblem on the door said Valle Escondido Police Department. There were no shady parking spaces here, so Drake volunteered to stay with Rusty and let him out for a run.

Inside, the one story building was split in two by a hallway running from the front door to the back. The first door on my right had a small plastic sign above it, the kind that sticks out into the hallway, hanging from a metal bracket. It said ADMINISTRATIVE OFFICES. Directly across the hall was an identical arrangement with the words POLICE DEPARTMENT.

I opened the door, which had wavy opaque glass in the top half, to find myself facing a long counter. The formica top had once been white, but was now covered with ink streaks, scratches, and carved initials. No one was in sight. I tapped once on a silver metal bell that had been placed on the counter for my convenience. The Chief himself answered.

Steve Bradley was fifty-ish with blond hair going silver, tall, and probably good-looking except for the extra forty pounds he carried, mostly around the middle. He wore his dark uniform shirt open at the collar, showing the neck of a white undershirt and a sprouting of chest hair above it. He carried a clipboard and appeared to be in motion, like he hadn't yet found a chance to sit down today. I identified him by the collar insignia words "Chief" flanking his neck.

"Chief Bradley," I said, "I'm Charlie Parker, from Albuquerque."

His eyebrows went upward in a silent question.

"An acquaintance here in Valle Escondido was a friend of Cynthia Martinez. I understand there have been some questions about her death."

His face remained polite, but I could see he had no intention of telling me anything of importance.

"My friend was at the funeral. She also said you came to her house this morning. Laura Armijo."

"Yeah, well," he said, "I guess she told you Richard Martinez caused a little stink at the funeral. Figured I better find out what happened." His voice was soft, discreet, with an accent that hinted slightly at West Texas.

"Has anyone filed a complaint against him?" I asked.

"Nope."

"Laura doesn't seem to think Cynthia's death was just an unfortunate coincidence."

"Laura doesn't *want* to think so," he said. He crossed to the dispatcher's desk behind the counter and set the clipboard down.

He breathed heavily as he lowered himself into the swivel chair. "Ya see, Laura was in the same condition herself about a year or so ago, and she lost her baby too. Cynthia was her good friend, and this all hits a little too close to home for Laura's taste." The man was perceptive anyway.

"Did you know the Martinezes personally?" I asked.

"In a town this size, I know most everyone," he answered. "I either went to school with 'em, or one of my younger brothers did, or one of my sisters babysat 'em. Twenty years on the department has brought me together with just about everybody here at some time."

I could well believe that.

"What about Barbara Lewis? I hear she was pretty tough to work for."

"They call her the office witch," he chuckled. He had a laugh like an old choo-choo train just starting off. "Barbara's about my age, couple years younger, I think. She grew up in a time when women were raised to believe they'd become wives and mothers, and some man would take care of them. She fit right into that cozy little picture until Archie Lewis ran off with his secretary about ten years ago."

"And there she was, forty-something, no work experience, having to support herself," I filled in.

"And three kids. She realized that she'd never make it on minimum wage plus tips, so she went for the top. That bank manager's job is one of the best in town."

"Not easy to get, either, I'd imagine, having no work experience."

"Well, Barbara's a fighter. You oughta go talk to her. You'll see."

"Where would I find her on a Saturday?"

He thought about it for a minute. "Odds are, she'll be home. That, or at the grocery store."

He proceeded to tell me how to get to Barbara Lewis's house. Drake and Rusty were waiting under the covered porch, in the only strip of shade to be seen anywhere, when I came out. Again, I felt guilty for being inside while they dealt with the heat.

"Don't worry about it," Drake assured me. "We found lots to do. We made lunch plans. Are you hungry?"

I tend to forget about food when I get busy, so I hadn't given it much thought. A glance at my watch, though, told me it was after one.

"Okay, you two, what are the plans?" I asked. I didn't want to leave Rusty in the car again, and Drake and I hadn't discussed whether we would stay overnight.

"There's a take-out chicken place about two blocks from here," he said. "We're going to get a big bucket with all the trimmings, and then we're going to that little park next to the hardware store. You and I are going to find a big shady spot under a tree, and Rusty's going to do whatever he wants."

What a sweetheart. He'd thought of all our needs.

"How did you know about the take-out chicken place?" I asked.

He walked his fingers along the dashboard, then pointed to a pay phone mounted to the corner of the building. A man with a plan. I liked that.

Thirty minutes later I was licking the grease from my fingers, leaning back against a tree trunk. Drake lay stretched out on the blanket he'd found in the back of my Jeep, which I'd forgotten was in there. Rusty had been hand fed the meat from two pieces of extra crispy, then allowed to lick the remains from the mashed potato container. Our cholesterol levels were buzzing, and somnolence was beginning to overtake all three of us.

"I just can't quite put this together," I told Drake.

"Not surprising, since you're almost asleep," he mumbled.

I stood up and stretched, just to prove that I could. His pessimism about my current mental capacity wasn't going to stop me.

"Just listen a minute, and tell me what you think."

He yawned, to warn me that I might not get much out of him either.

"The doctor at the clinic confirmed that Cynthia died after she miscarried. Richard seems pretty broken up about her death. He caused a little scene at the funeral, and now the police are asking questions."

"So?"

"That's what I mean. So what? Why am I here?"

"Because your friend Sally and her friend Laura think there's more to it than that. Because you tend to agree with them. Because, my love, you are an incurable snoop."

I straddled his stomach and threatened to sit on him. He groaned.

"I just meant that you have this wonderful insatiable curiosity," he pleaded quickly.

"I was pretty sure that's what you meant," I answered, planting a couple of kisses on his fantastic mouth.

13

Barbara Lewis wasn't home. After working out in my mind what my questions would be, this was a letdown. Drake suggested we wait for her, in case she'd just gone to do morning errands. But I pointed out that the newspaper was still on the step, all the shades were drawn, and her porchlight was on. Looked like she had been gone overnight. Guess our trusty police chief didn't know everything.

"So, what now?" I asked. "Do we want to stay here overnight or head back to the big city?"

"Well, I had a feeling that question might come up, so I did a little more . . ." his fingers did that walking movement again.

"And?"

"Just drive," he ordered.

He pulled a scrap of paper from his back pocket as we fastened our seat belts.

"Okay, go north out of town," he said.

He didn't say another word as I guided the Jeep through the narrow streets. On the main road, traffic was fairly heavy as Saturday shoppers and errand runners did their rounds. Curiosity was consuming me, probably part of my inborn snoopiness, but I couldn't bring myself to pester Drake for the answer. He stared out the window, taking in the little town's sights as we cruised through. As the buildings began to thin out and the flat farmland become more prevalent, he consulted the paper once more.

"Okay now we want to watch for Lilac Lane," he said.

Lilac Lane? How quaint could we get? "Left or right?" was what I said out loud.

"Right."

It was about a half mile out of town. There wasn't a single lilac bush in sight. Lilac Lane was two-lane dirt and rather curvy, so I concentrated on the driving. We were climbing into the foothills now, the road rising steadily with every curve. The pines became taller, the grass greener. Daisies and columbine grew along the roadway in sporadic clumps. Occasional houses, some adobe and some log, sat back from the roadway, each in the middle of its own mowed patch of grass surrounded by tall pines. Drake watched the scenery go past, a relaxed smile on his face.

"Are you paying attention to the directions?" I reminded.

"There will be a little bridge up here soon," he said, "then we go three tenths of a mile past that."

The little bridge had concrete abutments with the date 1927. It spanned a small stream where clear water trickled over glossy pebbles. On the upstream side a log had fallen, creating a mini waterfall. I noted the mileage.

"Right hand side," he said. "Look for a narrow driveway."

It was marked by an entrance arch made of logs. A small discreet sign said Wildflower Inn: A Bed & Breakfast. Beyond a curve in the driveway, we could see the house, a log cabin, two stories high with dormer windows and European lace curtains. A wide porch ran the entire width of the house. Groupings of chairs and tables invited. Planter boxes thick with columbine lined the porch, while the upstairs windows had boxes of pink and white geraniums spilling from them. It was the best of northern New Mexico, Colorado mining camp, and Switzerland—all put together.

"Drake, this is wonderful!" Again, the resourceful man. How had he found this place?

Our tires crunched over a layer of fallen pine needles as we parked. Two dogs, young collies, rushed out to greet us.

"What about Rusty?" I asked.

"The lady said as long as he gets along with her dogs, no problem. I couldn't picture Rusty not getting along with anyone," he said, "so I took the chance."

We got out, keeping Rusty on a leash until we knew what would happen with the other dogs. They sniffed each other all over, then the other two strolled back toward the house. No worries. Meanwhile, a woman had come out the front door, drying her hands on a dish towel. She was probably forty-five or so, with shoulder length dark hair with a swoop of gray sprouting from the part on the left side. Her face was lined with the beginnings of character wrinkles, like she'd been an outdoor person all her life. She wore faded jeans with a hole across one knee and a loose plaid shirt, tucked in at the waist, sleeves rolled up to the elbows.

"Welcome. You must be Drake," she said, extending her hand to him. "And Charlie." She took me into her welcoming hug.

"I'm Mary McDonald. Welcome to the Wildflower."

I was still staring at my surroundings, still taking in the beauty of the place.

"I'm amazed we got in on such short notice," I said.

"You got lucky," she said. "I had a cancellation just yesterday. I've only got three rooms here, and I'm usually booked all summer. But this couple from Canada—the airline got their connecting flight into Albuquerque messed up. Poor things, they're spending the weekend in Chicago. Can you imagine anything worse?"

I had to admit that their misfortune was our stroke of luck.

"Let me show you to your room," Mary continued. "Where are your bags?"

Inside, the cabin was just as lovely as outside. A large greatroom held several sofas and chairs, all overstuffed and comfy looking, upholstered in variations of navy and burgundy. On the wall to our left was a rock fireplace, its wooden mantle laden with a variety of multi-colored candles. The wall ahead was lined with bookcases holding an assortment of worn volumes along with decks of cards, dominoes, and board games. A round game table and four chairs stood in the corner.

To our right, the dining area held a long table with eight chairs. A colorful gingham runner decorated the length of the table, with low centerpieces of fresh wildflowers. Beyond, a swinging door stood open to the kitchen, where I got a glimpse of shining ceramic tile and a large commercial stove.

"Technically, we're a bed and breakfast here," Mary was saying, "but I usually make up a pot of stew or beans or something in the evening. Anyone who doesn't have other dinner plans is free to join me."

She proceeded toward the stairs. We followed, hesitating as Rusty began the climb.

"He's okay," she assured us. "As long as he's housebroken."

I assured her he was.

"I keep one room off limits to pets, just in case I get guests with allergies sometime. Mostly I just warn them up front that there are animals around. Most of them seem to like it."

Our room was homey and quaint. The queen size brass bed was covered with a handmade quilt. We were in a corner of the house, so we had windows on two sides, both valanced with Dutch lace. White half-shutters could be closed for privacy. The view out the back showed nothing but pine trees, tall and thick.

The other window looked toward the side yard, across an expanse of neatly mowed lawn to a small gazebo at the edge of the woods.

"I'll bring a bed up for Rusty," Mary said. "I keep a couple of them around, and I wash the covers between visitors, just like for the people." Her laugh reminded me of the little stream we'd crossed.

"Oh, dinner's at seven, if you're interested. If not, coffee's on at seven in the morning, breakfast at eight." She closed the door behind her.

Drake's arms came around me from behind, his face nuzzled my ear. His spicy aftershave went well with the room and the view.

"This would be a great place for a honeymoon," he murmured.

I felt myself tense up. "Drake, it's just . . ."

"Too soon. I know." His arms dropped heavily at his sides.

I turned to find him pulling things out of the small duffle we'd mutually packed. He set his shaving kit on the vanity with a plop.

"I'm going to check with Mary about that dog bed," I said.

He hadn't turned around when I closed the door behind me. Rusty padded along with me, sniffing corners. I didn't see Mary in either the living room or kitchen, but that had been an excuse anyway. No one else was in sight, so I walked out to the front porch. The cushioned chairs looked inviting, but I wasn't able somehow to think about sitting still. Walking was what I needed.

Rusty busied himself sniffing the woodpile at the side of the house, no doubt hot in pursuit of chipmunks, while I strolled across the lawn toward the gazebo.

Marriage. Why was I getting so defensive at the mere mention of it? Being over thirty and always single had never bothered me yet. I'd been jilted once, but that incident hadn't bothered me that much at twenty. Certainly it wasn't affecting me all these years later. The few times in the intervening years when someone had begun to act serious about me, I'd managed to lightly skirt away from the issue before the big M word had been mentioned. Was that what I was trying to do now? If so, why was I out here pacing the floor of the gazebo? Why hadn't I just laughed off Drake's remark and distracted him in bed?

Because Drake Langston was different than any other man I'd met before. I could actually imagine having him around all the time. I could remember how much I'd missed him when we were apart. And it was scaring me.

Scared is not a feeling I like. It's not something I'm accustomed to. I pride myself on being a modern independent female, who doesn't need anyone to make her life complete. And therein lies the problem. When Drake wasn't near me, I felt a big empty place. It left me feeling confused, and confusion is another feeling I don't like.

Rusty had given up his probing of the woodpile now, and I watched him circle the house toward the front door. Drake was standing at the end of the porch, looking at me. He descended the steps and walked my way. Rusty trotted along beside him. The late afternoon air had grown cooler now. Drake had put on a long-sleeved shirt. He carried my light jacket.

"Thought you might want this," he said, raising the jacket.

I rubbed my arms. The skin was cool.

He held the jacket up for me, and I turned around to slip my arms into the sleeves. His hands stroked my shoulders, trailing down my arms to my hands. He rested his face against my hair.

"Sweetheart, I didn't mean to upset you," he said gently. "I won't mention it again until you're ready."

Tears welled up in my eyes, and I turned to bury my face against his shoulder until I could make them go away. Why didn't he push me? Then I could push back, and I could justify that I didn't need him after all. Why was he such an understanding guy?

"Let's walk a little while before dark," he suggested.

Rusty led the way down a narrow mountain path. Drake held my fingers lightly, pointing out a gray squirrel, then some elk tracks along the path. The tension was broken now. We were once again two people enjoying each other's company.

The path climbed to the left, circling behind the house, eventually bringing us back to the driveway. Another car was parked there now. By this time the sun had dropped below the hills, and the air had become nippy. A big fire blazed in the fireplace when we walked in, warming the large room to a golden coziness.

Mary introduced us to our fellow houseguests, Bob and Jean Braithwaite and Marvin and Bobbie Jo Connors. All from Lubbock, Texas. The women wore perfect makeup, designer jeans, and shirts with lots of fringe and spangles. Their hair was fluffed to within an inch of its life. Both men wore ostrich leather boots and Rolex watches with diamonds encrusted on the dials. I felt like a slightly well-to-do street person next to them.

"Well, ya'll, we're just on our way to town to check out the night life," Marvin Connors grinned. "Ya'll can join us if you want to."

Night life? In Valle Escondido? I had a feeling these people had taken a wrong turn at Santa Fe. I glanced up at Drake. Maybe I just imagined his nose turning up.

"Oh, no," he answered, "you go on. We'd kind of planned on a quiet evening by the fire."

Thank God. I couldn't imagine an evening with the glittering foursome.

They made some faux disappointment noises before tromping out the door. Jean Braithwaite's raucous laughter drifted back toward the house. I turned back toward Mary. Her earthy country presence was reassuring.

"*Ya'll* up for some green chile stew?" she mimicked with a wink.

"You bet," said Drake. "What can we do to help?" We followed her into the large kitchen.

"Why don't we just eat in here," she suggested, "since there are only three of us."

She handed plates to Drake, flatware and napkins to me. We set the small kitchen table while she lifted the lid on a large pot on the stove. The meaty, oniony smell filled the room. I excused myself to take Rusty upstairs. Poor thing. He'd have to settle for a bowl of dry nuggets while we indulged ourselves. I closed the door to the room, leaving him alone.

Drake was filling water glasses and Mary was placing corn-bread muffins in a cloth-lined basket when I returned. Steam rose from bowls of stew at each of the place settings.

"So, are you two honeymooners?" Mary asked, taking a careful sip of her stew.

I swallowed hard, hoping the moment wasn't about to become awkward. Drake covered it well, though.

"No," he said, "I'm here on vacation from Hawaii, and Charlie's investigating a suspicious case in town."

Mary didn't immediately ooh and aah over Hawaii like most people did, but looked questioningly at me.

"Well, it's unofficial," I said. "I'm a partner in a private investigation firm in Albuquerque. A friend here asked me to look into a suspicious death." I briefly mentioned the highlights of the case.

"I know Barbara Lewis," Mary said, breaking a cornbread muffin in two. "Went to school together. Valle Escondido High, class of sixty-eight."

"Really?"

"Barb was always real shy." She spread butter on the muffin and took a generous bite before speaking again. "She fell in love with Archie Lewis our sophomore year. Married him while she was still in high school. Had three kids, waited on that man hand and foot. Spent fifteen years doing that routine before Archie decided his secretary was a better deal."

She paused a minute to offer both of us more stew. Drake picked up the bowls and carried them to the stove for refills. I urged Mary to go on with her story.

"Candy was her name." She said it in a way that suggested uttering the word might give cavities. "She'd been a gangly little thing as a kid, then went off to Albuquerque to secretarial school, and came back polished as a diamond. Went right to work in Archie's car dealership. The girl must have known what she was doing. She was pregnant and married to Archie, in that order, before most of the town knew she was back."

"And Barbara?" I prompted.

"Barb was devastated. I swear she cried for months without stopping. She wallowed around that house, wearing this old cotton housecoat and never going out. I'd stop by to check on her and it was always the same. His picture was still on the shelf, some of his sports gear still in the garage. I think she was convinced that one day he'd see what a mistake he'd made, and he'd walk back in, suitcase in hand."

"Obviously, he didn't," Drake commented.

"Nope. When he and the chick had their new baby, the local paper ran a real cozy picture of the three of them. Extremely bad taste, if you ask me, considering the size of this town and the situation." She sniffed quickly. "I think that was Barb's turning point."

We had cleared the dishes by now and carried our coffee cups to the large sofa in front of the fire. Drake and I sat close together in one corner, while Mary took the matching print chair beside us.

"The next time I saw Barb," she continued, "she said she was on her way to Albuquerque. She came back a different person, in more ways than one. She had a new hairstyle, a new way of doing her makeup, and a whole new wardrobe. But the changes went deeper than that. She and I had lunch together one day, and she told me she was taking charge of her life. She was getting a job.

Archie had been good enough with the child support money, but Barb didn't want anything to do with him. Said she could support her own kids.

"The next thing I knew, she'd landed a job at the bank. Without any experience, I'm not sure how, but she did it. Worked hard, too. She kept pushing for the next higher position, until she became manager."

"I heard she's pretty hard on her people," I commented.

Mary shook her head sadly. "Yeah, that was the biggest change of all. Shy little Barbara Lewis apparently becomes this tiger lady on the job. It's weird, you know. I'd think she'd understand how it is to work your way up through the ranks, that she'd have a little sympathy for the underlings."

"What about on a personal level? Has your friendship survived?"

She smiled somewhat indulgently. "I understand a lot of things about people," she said. "Barb has built walls around herself, protective walls. I think, along with some others probably, that she's gone a bit too far with it. But she needs those walls right now. She went from being the most vulnerable kind of person to being so tough she's almost non-human. In time, I hope she'll find a middle ground somewhere, a place where she can be independent and still find room for love in her life. People need that, you know—independence and love."

Drake's arm around my shoulders didn't move an inch, but Mary's words struck home.

14

"What does this damned expense report mean!" I screamed.

"Don't yell, Charlie, Please don't yell anymore." I was sitting at my desk, and looked up to see Ron standing before me. His hair was white, his face wrinkled. I looked down at myself to find my own hands liver-spotted and wrinkled, my waist thick and my breasts saggy.

"Charlie?" Drake touched my shoulder and I awoke.

"I think you were having a bad dream," he whispered.

My eyes flew open; my breath came fast. Soft moonlight filtered through lace curtains. Drake was beside me, pulling the handmade quilt around my shoulders. Rusty's tags jingled in the corner of the room,

"You okay?" he asked again.

"Umm, yeah," I groaned, "I just had a weird dream." A piece of a dream, actually, a fragment of a hidden fear that I'd grow someday into the lonely, grouchy old office witch. I didn't tell him that.

He pulled me into the warm curve of his shoulder. His breathing became soft and regular within minutes. My mind whirled with unspoken thoughts for an eternity.

We both awoke with daylight in the unfamiliar room. It was still early. He rolled playfully toward me, and I wondered how much the strange bed would squeak. An hour later we snuggled once again into each other's arms, remembering that Mary had said breakfast was served at eight.

Our Texan housemates had come back last night around eleven, obviously disappointed with the night life in town. I could hear one pair of them now, shuffling around in the next room. Rusty curled into the corner bed that Mary had brought for him. He had ignored our lovemaking and seemed content enough with the status quo. We decided we could stay snuggled in for ten more minutes, then share a quick shower and still make it to breakfast.

Coffee smells drifted up the staircase as I walked down to let Rusty out. A large urn, flanked by a tray of mugs and pitchers of sugar, creamer, and artificial sweetener stood on the sideboard at one end of the large dining room. The two other women guests, no less perfect looking than the night before, sat in the living room. One of the husbands carried bags toward their car.

I heard our bedroom door open, so I poured two mugs of coffee, fixing one to Drake's taste. He appeared in the doorway a moment later.

"You folks leaving today?" I heard Drake ask Marvin Connors.

"Yeah, how about ya'll?"

"No, we're staying the weekend," Drake told him.

"Well, you have fun," Marvin replied. "We got a schedule to keep. Frankly," he said, only slightly lowering his voice, "I find this place a little *too* quiet."

I handed Drake his coffee, and we both turned toward the kitchen to see if we could give Mary a hand.

"No," she insisted, "you're guests. Besides, everything's ready. All I have to do is put it on the table."

Drake didn't wait for permission. He picked up a large pitcher of fresh orange juice, which he handed to me, then reached for the tray of covered plates Mary had just stacked on the counter.

Mary smiled as he turned toward the dining room. She nudged me. "That one's a keeper," she whispered. She pushed through the swinging door. I took a deep breath before I followed.

"Breakfast is ready," Mary announced to the other four guests. They pried themselves out of the deep sofas. Mary took the pitcher of orange juice from me and began filling glasses. Drake held my chair for me. Marvin Connors had practically leapt for the chair at the head of the table, leaving his wife standing. Drake circled the table and held a chair for her before taking his own seat. I smiled at him and squeezed his knee under the table.

I had hoped Mary would join us for breakfast, but as hostess it wasn't part of her duties. She busied herself back and forth from the kitchen, bringing more juice and a basket of warm flour tortillas. Breakfast was huevos rancheros, a favorite New Mexico concoction of tortilla, beans, eggs, and cheese. The tradition is to drown it in either red or green chile sauce, which Mary thoughtfully left to each guest's discretion. Drake and I both smothered ours in green chile, while the Texas guests dribbled on spots of red.

"So, Charlie, when do you usually get to Dallas?" drawled Jean Braithwaite.

"Excuse me?"

"For your spring shopping?" she answered. Sensing a blank, she fumbled. "You do come to Dallas for your spring wardrobe, don't you dear?"

Spring wardrobe? Right. I bought a new pair of shorts at Penneys last May, I think.

"I'm afraid not," I told her.

She and Bobbie Jo exchanged incredulous looks, and that conversation dropped flat. The husbands took up the slack, though. We heard all about how Marvin and Bob had bought this little oil business, and by virtue of their incredible business smarts had built it into a "real good little operation." They each had a lake house at Lake Texoma, and took ski vacations together in Red River, and of course they liked to turn the ladies loose in Dallas a couple of times a year to "buy themselves a few pretties." As if we hadn't noticed them, Marvin pointed out the matching Rolexes. I stifled a yawn, not too successfully, and noticed that Drake's eyes were glazing over.

Mary broke the monologue by asking whether anyone wanted more food, juice, or coffee.

"Excuse me," I said, "I better give Rusty his breakfast."

Drake stood up, too. "Maybe I should help."

We both collapsed in giggles as soon as our door was closed.

"I've been thinking," I said, when I could catch my breath. "Maybe I should have a makeover at Elizabeth Arden. Then I could re-think my image at Neiman Marcus."

"Don't you dare," he said, pulling me on top of him. "I like you exactly the way you are."

The conversation deteriorated into a series of long kisses, until we heard a car start up out front.

Downstairs, Mary had cleared the table, and was stacking plates in the dishwasher.

"No, you're not going to help again," she said, just as Drake opened his mouth to volunteer. "Here, get another cup of coffee and pull up a chair at the kitchen table.

"What do you have planned for the day?" she asked, once we settled in our seats.

"I'd like to ask some more questions around town," I told her. "I feel like I've been goofing off a lot. Although, this being Sunday, I may have a hard time finding the people I need to see."

I told her we'd tried to find Barbara Lewis at home the previous day, with no luck. "It looked like she'd gone out of town."

She finished the dishes, and dried her hands on a towel.

"Barbara would probably be back this afternoon, even if she was out of town. Work tomorrow, you know. I could call her for you, if you'd like."

I thought showing up unannounced would more likely net me some unrehearsed answers, so I just told Mary I'd think about it.

"Did you know Cynthia Martinez?" I asked.

"Just slightly. She used to come out here and buy eggs from me." She poured herself a cup of coffee and joined us at the table, letting out a groan as she sat. "I kept chickens when I first moved out here, you see. But, it was a hassle. The winters up here in the hills get pretty cold. I lost the whole batch of 'em the first winter, The next year I tried again, but it was a lot of work and not much reward. People are too lazy to drive this far out for a dozen eggs, especially when they can just pick them up at the supermarket in town. Doesn't matter that fresh eggs are so much better.

"Anyway, Cynthia used to come out. She has some family up the road from here, so she was driving up this way anyhow."

"Did you get friendly with her?" I asked.

"Oh, yeah. Friendly, but not close, you know."

"Did she talk about wanting a baby?"

"Constantly. She was pregnant, too. Last spring, a year ago. Yeah, that's the last time I had any chickens. She was so careful, too. I mean, she really watched everything she ate. Part of the reason she came here for eggs, because mine have never been tainted. I remember one time she came by and had this terrible headache, you know, so bad that she was kinda squinting her eyes shut. I offered her some aspirin, but she wouldn't have it. Because of the baby. Even Tylenol. Wouldn't take that because she said she was allergic." She held her hands around the coffee cup for warmth. "Yes, that woman was careful."

"Did you ever hear rumors that her husband beat her?"

"No!" Mary seemed genuinely surprised. "Of course, we weren't that close. Cynthia was cordial, but she didn't open up about the baby. She wouldn't have told me anything bad about her husband."

"The doctor seemed to dismiss the idea entirely," I mentioned.

Mary tightened up. "Hmpf. Those doctors in town. Couldn't get me to one of them for anything. I see an herbalist when I need some little cure."

"What if something really serious came up?"

"Well, if I found out I had cancer or something, I'd go to Santa Fe or Albuquerque. Not here."

"Why not?"

"Hell, I went to school with Evan Phillips. Babysat for Rodney Phillips when I was in junior high." She chuckled good-naturedly. "I guess I'd just have a hard time undressing for either of them."

"What else can you tell me about the town, or the people?" I asked.

"Oh, gosh, I don't know," she answered. "I've been here so long, nothing about this place seems unique to me. You want history about the town, you could try the library or the museum."

"There's a museum here?"

"The Miner's Museum. It's down on Potts Street, about a block off the plaza. Just drive down to the plaza, northwest corner, then wander. You can't miss it."

I couldn't imagine what a museum exhibit would have to do with the Cynthia Martinez problem, but I'm a sucker for learning about old stuff. Besides, it would be a way to kill a few hours before we tried once again to drop in on Barbara Lewis.

"Would it be a problem for Rusty to stay here while we go to town?" I asked.

"Not a bit," she assured me. "You take as long as you want. He's a good boy, and he gets along fine with my two."

The temperature rose by several degrees as we descended from the cool mountain valley into town. Cars lined the main street, the thickest clump of them outside the Catholic church. They radiated outward from that hub, parking down side streets as well. Another cluster surrounded Rosa's Cantina. We headed for the plaza, where we had no trouble finding a parking place. Drake took my hand as we strolled the quiet street, glancing in shop windows.

From each corner of the plaza, narrow winding side streets radiated out like threads raveling off a patch of cloth. I had no idea which corner was northwest, but we were in no hurry and the plaza wasn't that large. We wandered until we found it.

The Miner's Museum was packaged in a small wooden building skirted by a wooden plank sidewalk. A narrow shingled roof, supported by sturdy wood poles and braced by an honest-to-goodness hitching post extended over the walkway. Based on the scars in the wood, I guessed that the hitching post had, at one time, been functional. A small plaque beside the door announced that the museum was supported by donations and gave the hours. It was due to open in ten minutes, so Drake and I settled onto a weathered wooden bench beside the door.

Precisely eight minutes later, we saw the man approach. Somewhere around eighty years of age, he walked with only a slight stoop in his shoulders and an almost lively spring in his step. His pure white hair showed pink scalp beneath, and his lips formed a straight line that angled downward at one corner.

"Howdy." The single word came out of the low corner of his mouth.

His watery-looking eyes sparkled, and the straight mouth opened into a grin full of perfect dentures. He pulled a key attached to a bright green plastic keyring from his pocket, and aimed it toward the lock on the ancient doorknob.

"You folks waiting on me?" he inquired. Again, the words came from the corner of the mouth. He grinned again when we nodded.

"Well, come on in," he invited. "Just take me a minute to get the lights turned on."

We stepped inside as he held the door wide. His gnarled hand fumbled for a switch on the wall somewhere out of sight behind the door. Fluorescent lights flickered a moment before they glowed steadily. The walls of the small room were weathered wood, like they'd been taken off an old barn somewhere. Doorways to our left and right led to other unseen rooms. In front of us stood a desk, with a none-too-discreet sign stating that admission was free, but that a donation of two dollars per person would be appreciated.

"Now, just a minute here, and I'll get this all ready for you," the old man mumbled.

He patted the wall in the darkened room to our left, searching for the light switch. After about six or seven pats, the room lit up. Shuffling across to the other dark room on the right, he repeated the procedure. Then he made his way slowly to the desk and sat heavily in the chair behind it, breathing deeply. He pulled the center drawer open and bent his white head low, eyes and hands searching the contents for something. At last he pulled a white plastic-encased card from the drawer and pinned it laboriously to his shirt pocket. Bart Johnson, Miner's Museum, was hand lettered in wavery black ink on the name tag. When he had straightened it to his satisfaction, Bart looked back up at us.

"The tour is self-guided," he said. "There are displays in both the side rooms. Just take your time."

Drake had pulled a five dollar bill from his wallet, and told Bart to keep the change. The old man grinned again crookedly. I glanced at Drake as we entered the room on the right, and he winked at me.

The chronology of the little museum was a bit confusing, as it didn't seem there was much method to the displays. One wall held a collection of mining tools, mounted at interesting angles with nails on the wooden wall. A small cart with railroad wheels stood in the corner, filled with dirt and rocks representing the loot they used to haul out of the hills.

The opposite wall was covered with framed photographs and small hand lettered signs outlining the history of the mining days in the valley. I was surprised to learn that gold and silver had been among the big finds here. Photo groupings of men in dusty overalls, solemn faces caked with black, showed that the life wasn't an easy one. There were few women in the pictures.

One woman who was probably twenty, but looked forty, sat in a rocker on a front porch very similar to the one on this building. A chubby-faced infant sat on her lap, while two other children under the age of three clung to her skirts and stared with large dark eyes at the stranger who photographed them. No one in any of the pictures smiled.

A placard inserted between some of the photos showed a crude map of the town, then and now. Different colored markers indicated the portions attributed to different periods in time. The plaza was shown in brown and the color key indicated that it dated back to Spanish exploration days. Small red squares on the periphery showed the location of the mining camp, dated 1885. Those buildings drawn in dotted lines no longer existed, which was almost all of them. Only one red building, named here as Phillips Mercantile, remained. There were two photos of it, then and now. "Then" showed a large stone building, three stories tall with dark slim arched windows; "Now" merely an empty roofless shell.

Apparently the mining operation thrived for close to fifty years, but inevitably vanished. The gold and silver veins had given out and the people moved on. In its heyday, the town's population had been around nine thousand. When the miners left it dwindled back to the two thousand or so level where it remains today.

We wandered back through the middle room, startling Bart Johnson out of a little snooze. He grinned crookedly and immediately became busy straightening postcards on the rack at his desk.

"Enjoying the museum?" he asked.

"I had no idea there was a mining operation of this scale up here, " I told him.

"Yep, they took out over forty million dollars worth."

"So many of the old mining towns in New Mexico just vanished after their mines closed down, though. Valle Escondido seems to be one of the few towns still going strong," I observed.

He scratched behind his left ear. "Well, you know this town was here a long time before them miners came. Spanish explorers got here first, I guess. Then the frontiersmen, Kit Carson and his cronies. There was even a Civil War battle fought just up the road here."

"Glorietta Pass," I said. "I've heard of it."

"Lot of old families here," he continued, shaking his white head slowly. "Yep, lot of old bitterness."

I wondered what he meant by that, but he suddenly became busy again, folding and straightening some brochures.

The third room contained firearms in glass cases, labelled with small signs indicating where they had been found or who they'd belonged to. A couple of dress forms displayed clothing worn by the townspeople. The dresses were made of sturdy material, tattered now with patched places and frayed edges. Nothing of the Hollywood western image here. The whole place conveyed not a sense of adventure and glamour, but of sadness.

15

"Want some lunch?" Drake asked as we stepped out onto the creaky wooden porch once more.

"We could sample the enchiladas, or maybe a burrito at Rosa's, then see if Barbara Lewis is back in town," I suggested.

Rosa's was jammed with the after church crowd. We stood in line twenty minutes before getting a table, but it proved worth the wait. The steaming plates of enchiladas smothered in gooey cheese arrived quickly. I wondered whether Drake might be getting tired of all the Mexican food we'd been eating, but he seemed to relish it. People were still waiting for tables when we finished, so we paid the check and left.

A spotless blue Volvo stood in the driveway at Barbara Lewis's house. The porch light was off and the newspapers had been picked up. She answered the door almost immediately.

Barbara Lewis was fifty-ish with dark hair generously streaked with gray, cut severely in a masculine style. She stood a firm five foot four in a body that looked like she had to fight to keep it from spreading south. She wore black stirrup pants and a black and white geometric patterned tunic sweater, obviously a professional color coordination job to go with her hair. Burgundy lipstick gave her mouth an unyielding look, although that might have been enhanced by the two deep crevices between the black eyebrows. Her brown eyes, rather than her mouth, asked what we wanted.

"Ms. Lewis? I wonder if we might talk to you for a few moments."

She moved as if to close the door, and I realized that I must have sounded like a survey taker.

"It's about Cynthia Martinez," I explained, rummaging in my purse for a business card.

She studied the card, ready at any moment to shut the door in our faces.

"Mary McDonald suggested that I talk to you."

She loosened up noticeably, but didn't quite let go of a smile. "May we come in?"

She didn't want to let us, but couldn't think of a graceful way to refuse after the mention of her friend's name. She stepped aside, keeping one hand on the edge of the door, while we squeezed past.

Inside, the living room was arranged with precision, although lacking the sophistication of Barbara's personal appearance. Early American chairs flanked a matching sofa. Maple end tables and coffee table each held one or two objects, a lamp here, a candy dish there. Nothing looked like it was allowed to move from its assigned spot. The carpet was orange and brown variegated shag. The walls were decorated with small mass-production paintings, the kind found at starving artists sales. No imagination, but not quite tacky. The room probably looked exactly as it had fifteen years earlier when Archie Lewis had decided he'd become bored with his life.

"I understand you were Cynthia's supervisor at work," I began after we'd perched ourselves on the edge of the sofa,

"That's right," Barbara had sealed herself to one of the large chairs, her rear also near the front edge. Clearly, no one was going to relax just yet.

"Can you tell me what happened that last Friday when she died?"

"Nothing at the bank was unusual, if that's what you mean," she said. "Cynthia showed up for work late. Said she'd been to a doctor's appointment. As I remember, she didn't look very well. She was away from her desk quite a lot." Her face conveyed severe disapproval.

"Did she say she was ill?"

"Obviously she was ill."

How could I be so stupid?

Barbara continued: "After the third trip to the bathroom, I suggested that she might as well go home, as she wasn't doing anyone any good in her present condition."

"Did she say she was bleeding?"

"My girls don't dump their personal problems on me," she said shortly.

Dump their personal problems? I felt my blood pressure rising.

"So she went home after that?" Drake asked.

Barbara at least had the good grace to squirm a little now. "Well," she hesitated, "she worked most of the afternoon. But she fainted."

"And then what?"

"One of the girls called an ambulance. We got the call a few hours later that she'd had a miscarriage and died." She stated it so matter-of-factly that I couldn't believe this was a co-worker she was talking about.

"At least you went to the funeral," I said. I could hear the sarcasm in my own voice, despite an effort to keep it out.

"I think that's about all I care to say on the matter," she answered, standing. Clearly, we were being dismissed.

Outside, I exhaled through my teeth before trusting myself to speak. "Can you believe that!"

Drake guided me toward the Jeep. He didn't say anything until he had me safely in the passenger seat. He reached for my keys and started the car. Two blocks away, he pulled into the grocery store parking lot, cut the engine, and turned to me. I slid across to his open arms.

"People are really hard to figure out, aren't they?" he said gently.

Tears stung my eyes. I squeezed them tightly shut to avoid making a total fool of myself. Why do I do this to myself? Why do I have this sympathetic spot for people I don't even know? For one crazy minute I considered what it might be like to pack a suitcase and run off to Hawaii with Drake, forgetting this little northern New Mexico town and Sally's friend and the fact that a woman had died mysteriously. Why didn't I just do it?

Because something about Barbara Lewis had come across as so cold and unfeeling that I wanted to nail the woman. I couldn't see how she could have been directly responsible for Cynthia's death, but that was beside the point. Right now, I was angry. I almost understood how Richard Martinez had lost his temper at the funeral. I almost believed him.

Almost, but not quite. I sat up straight again.

"What if Cynthia was late for work that day, not because of a doctor appointment but because her husband was in a rage?"

Drake looked at me, not speaking, encouraging me to go on with my thoughts.

"What if he had beat her that morning?"

"Wouldn't the doctors have found bruises? Evidence of a beating?" He interjected rationality into the conversation.

"Okay. That makes sense. Then, what is Barbara Lewis hiding?"

He didn't have an answer for that one. We both sat silently staring out the window. My mind raced. I needed to figure out what Cynthia had done that morning, what steps had eventually led to her being taken away in an ambulance.

"Let's go talk to Laura Armijo again," I suggested. "You drive."

Laura greeted us warmly and offered iced tea as soon as we stepped into her home.

"If you don't mind, let's talk in the kitchen," she said. "I'm putting a roast into the oven for dinner tonight."

Drake and I took seats on barstools at the counter. Laura's energetic movements were almost tiring to the observer.

"I'm so glad you're still here," she told us. "At least someone is taking the time to investigate this."

"I'm not sure that I'm doing a wonderful job for you," I answered. "So far, I haven't found anyone who doesn't seem to believe that Cynthia just died of complications from the miscarriage."

"Technically that might be true, Charlie. But what caused the miscarriage? I can't believe she lost two babies in two years just by chance. I still think Richard had something to do with it."

"Tell me what happened that Friday at work. You didn't learn of Cynthia's death until Sunday when Sally and I were here. Didn't someone call the bank on Friday with the news?"

"They might have. I had Friday off. I'd gone to Santa Fe for some shopping. Bobby decided to join me there that night, and we stayed over at the Inn of the Governors. We got back Saturday night late."

"I'd like to talk to someone else from the bank who would have been there Friday."

"Barbara Lewis?"

"I tried that." I guess my expression told her how that went.

"How about Jennifer Lang? She's one of the tellers." Laura paused a moment from sprinkling seasoning salt on the roast. Her eyes looked upward. "She's . . . how should I say this . . . talkative."

Not too discreet. Good. Maybe we'd get the real skinny on the situation.

"Shall I call her for you?" Laura offered.

"No, I'd rather just drop in. Can you give me directions to her house?"

Ten minutes later, we were on our way. Heavy clouds had begun to accumulate over the mountains. A sporadic breeze stirred up dust devils, whipping bits of leaves and debris upward in spirals. The temperature hadn't dropped a bit, though. Now the air felt like a soggy wool blanket over our heads.

Jennifer Lang's apartment was on the main street, a twenty year old ten-plex, stuccoed pale tan with peeling turquoise paint on the trim and stair railings. Her place was on the second floor. The turquoise door was in a little better shape than some. I pounded at it, I hoped firmly enough to be heard over the rock music blasting behind it.

Jennifer swung the door open quickly, like she'd been expecting someone. Her eyes registered surprise to see strangers. Dark permed hair flowed wildly around her shoulders. She pushed an unruly strand back from her forehead. Her dark eyes were made up in three colors, and she had an upturned nose and full mouth. She wore red plaid men's boxer shorts, the elastic at the top rolled down a couple of turns, and a skin tight red tank top — nothing else. The outline of her nipples was almost distracting. I glanced at Drake. Yes, definitely distracting.

"Hi, Jennifer, I'm Charlie Parker. Laura Armijo suggested we stop by and talk to you."

"Laura? From the bank?" She glanced backward into the apartment. "Uh, sure, come on in."

She backed away, giving us space, closing the door behind us and turning the music down.

"Oh, just a second. Let me move some stuff here." She scooped up an armful of magazines from the sofa and dumped them on the floor beside it. We sat, sinking at odd angles on springs that had quit working years earlier. Jennifer took the only chair, one of those rattan round things that look impossible to get in or out of. She didn't bother moving the socks, blouse, or pantyhose draped over it.

"Laura has asked us to look into Cynthia Martinez's death," I began. "She wasn't at work that day, but said you were. Maybe you could tell us what happened."

"Well, yeah, I guess so," she said.

"Cynthia came in late, I hear."

"Yeah, she'd gone to her doctor appointment. You know, when you're pregnant you have to go a lot. Like every month or so."

I nodded. Drake was making a conscious effort not to stare at her chest.

"Well, she'd been doing that ever since she got pregnant. She was really excited about that baby. I don't think her husband wanted it so much, but Cynthia — well, she'd really have been a good mom, you know."

"Was she having trouble with the pregnancy?"

"I don't think so. I mean, she never mentioned anything, you know. She just went to the doctor every month. And she was really careful about what she ate. You know, she brought all this healthy stuff for lunch every day? And she wouldn't even have a beer after work, like the rest of us did sometimes."

"What about that Friday? Was she feeling bad?"

"Yeah, she didn't look right all morning. She came in after her doctor appointment, but she just didn't look right."

"How do you mean?"

"Well, she told me she had this pounding headache. She woke up with it, and she said the doctor had given her something for it. But it didn't go away. Then, right after lunch she came out of the bathroom, and she told one of the other girls she had bad cramps and was bleeding. I mean, that's not right, is it?" She glanced at Drake, embarrassed. "You're not supposed to you know, when you're pregnant?"

"I don't think so," I told her. "What happened after that? Did she call her doctor?"

"I got busy, so I'm not sure, but I don't think so. She went to lie down in the employee lounge for awhile. Then Ms. Lewis was storming around looking for her, and she came back to her desk. There were customers waiting, you know. I mean, you can't imagine how crazy the bank is on Friday afternoons." Her eyes rolled upward to convey the pressure she was under at work.

"Then what?"

"Well, I looked over at her a couple of times, and I thought she really looked pale. And kind of sweaty. She went in the restroom a few more times, and Ms. Lewis was getting really pissed. I mean, you can just tell it, you know, She doesn't even have to say anything, but she gets this look."

Jennifer squinted her eyebrows together tightly in a pretty good imitation of Barbara Lewis's perpetual scowl.

"Like that? Well, anyway, she's giving that look to Cynthia all afternoon, until finally about three o'clock, Cynthia just passed out. I mean, right there on the floor."

She patted her chest, her eyes wide now. "It really scared all of us, Ms. Lewis wanted us to take her into the lounge and put a cold cloth on her face, but the other girls were worried. I mean, after what Cynthia told us about the cramps and all. So someone called 911. The ambulance came right away. I don't know if they took her to the clinic or to Santa Fe. I never heard. They called about five to say that she had died."

"Did you go to the funeral?" I asked.

"No, we had to keep the bank open. Ms. Lewis went, and some of the other girls. Actually, I volunteered to work. I hate funerals, ever since this one guy in our class in high school was killed in a car wreck and we all had to go to the funeral. It was so sad."

She stared at the carpet, her soft young features still now. I knew what she meant. I'd attended my parent's double funeral when I was sixteen. I hate the whole business, too.

Drake broke the silence with a discreet clearing of the throat. I couldn't think of any other questions for Jennifer. I handed her my card, and asked her to call me if she thought of anything else that might explain why a seemingly healthy pregnant woman would suddenly miscarry and die. We walked again into the heavy heat outside.

"I think you'd look cute in an outfit like that," Drake grinned, once we'd reached the car.

I glanced sideways at him. "Really?" Flatterer. At least his attentions were not easily stolen by a twenty year old with a fantastic body.

Suddenly, I was tired. The late afternoon sun had gone behind the deepening clouds, giving the impression that it was almost dusk.

"Let's go back to the Wildflower," I said.

"You hungry yet?" he asked.

"Not very." I really didn't want to think about food yet. But it didn't seem right to expect Mary to feed us again. After all, we were only supposed to get breakfast in the deal.

"Why don't we call her and see if we can bring a pizza back for all of us?" he suggested.

He started the Jeep, and headed back up the main street. Pulling in at a pizza place, he found a phone and made the call. I watched from the car, thinking about the day, mulling over the interviews we'd done. Some answers were in there someplace. I just didn't know where.

Drake stepped away from the pay phone and flashed me a thumbs up. He disappeared inside the pizza place, apparently to place an order. A few minutes later, he came back out.

"It'll take about twenty minutes for the pizza," he said. "Want to come inside and have something to drink? They've got fairly comfortable looking booths in there."

A wine cooler sounded good, but I knew it would make me sleepy. I settled for a Coke. Drake had a light beer. The time passed quickly enough, and I felt somewhat rejuvenated by the time we arrived at Mary's.

Raindrops splatted on the dry ground as we drove up. By the time we got inside the water was coming down in sheets.

"You guys made it just in time," Mary greeted, holding the screen door open for us. "I've got a fire going, and a bottle of wine open. Our other guests may not make it. They called from Albuquerque to say they'd just arrived. If they get here at all, it'll be late."

Rusty was overjoyed to see us. He rubbed against my legs, and licked Drake's fingers thoroughly. I promised him a pizza crust if he'd lie down in the corner while we ate. We sat around the coffee table in front of the fire. This time I didn't worry whether the wine would make me sleepy. The rain on the roof, the warm fire, the occasional thunder in the distance all had a lulling effect. Mary vanished discreetly after the pizza was gone, leaving Drake and me alone with the fire. He pulled me into the curve of his arm, not talking, just being there. I forced myself not to remember that he'd be leaving again in three days.

16

Our lovemaking the next morning had an almost desperate quality. Like we both realized our time together was almost over, and we wanted to extract everything we could from the time we had left. I was having a hard time with this. The idea of committing to move in together, or more drastically, to get married, hadn't settled with me yet. But the idea of watching him leave again, of knowing that it would be months, if ever, before we were together again . . . I couldn't accept that, either.

The quilts were warm, Drake's body comforting, as I drifted in and out of cozy sleep. The house was devoid of sound. Apparently the other guests had never come in. Breakfast was not a pressing matter. If we missed it, fine. Somehow I thought Mary sensed our situation, though, and would keep the meal waiting.

Drake stirred next to me, and I realized he was wide awake. When I mumbled incoherently into his chest, my voice awakened Rusty. He had pressing matters on his mind. Like it or not, I had to get up. Wrapping my terry robe around myself, I fumbled my way to the door and down the stairs, Rusty eager at my heels. He raced out into the yard the second the door opened.

Coffee makings waited on the sideboard, and discreet sounds of pans clanking together came from the kitchen. I glanced at my watch. It was after ten. Poor Mary, if she wanted to run on a schedule around here, we had certainly messed it up for her.

"Sorry we're so lazy this morning," I said, poking my head into the kitchen.

She grinned indulgently. "No problem. Those other people didn't make it last night. Good thing I got a deposit from them, because I imagine there will be an argument over weather delays being someone's fault."

I apologized again and told her we'd be down soon.

The shower was running when I entered our room, and I could hear Drake whistling something from a Broadway musical. I dropped my robe and joined him under the hot spray.

Fifteen minutes later, dried and dressed, we quickly threw our few belongings into the duffle we'd brought. I glanced back at the brass bed, the homemade quilts and white shutters. The weekend had been a wonderful getaway, despite the fact that I was there to work.

Downstairs, Drake carried the bag out to the car, while I offered to help Mary organize breakfast. Within minutes, Drake's footsteps clomped loudly across the porch.

"Charlie, come out here," he called out.

Something in his voice alerted me. I felt the hair on my arms rise.

"We've got trouble," he said through the screen. "Have Mary call the police."

"What! Where's Rusty?"

"He's fine," Drake answered almost impatiently. "There's been some vandalism to the Jeep."

I pushed the screen outward. "My Jeep? My almost new Jeep?"

"What's going on?" Mary had come up behind me.

"Our fuel line has been slashed," Drake informed us. His mouth was set in a firm line.

"Oh, my God," Mary said quietly. She finished drying her hands on a dish towel, striding quickly toward the vehicle.

Sure enough, the smell of gasoline grew stronger as we approached. I turned to Drake.

"Are you sure it was deliberately cut?"

He raised the hood and showed us the spot. A neat slice bisected the line near the fuel injector.

"It obviously wasn't a pro," Drake said. "He cut such a large gash that the line drained immediately. If he'd wanted to make it look accidental, he should have made a small hole. Then the gas would have been pumped up here and come out in spurts. As we drove, and the engine heated up, it probably would have caused a good-sized fire." His mouth was grim.

My stomach felt like lead.

"I'm calling Steve Bradley," Mary said, firmly. "Nothing like this has ever happened out here." She marched back toward the house.

I stared at the crippled Jeep, my only emotion—disbelief. When and how had this happened? Why hadn't any of the dogs alerted us to the intruder?

Footprints surrounded the Jeep in the soft mud, but they were vague and indistinguishable. Probably made by overshoes, smooth on the bottom. The area where the vehicle was parked consisted of dirt, gravel, and grass. Prints just didn't show well.

I walked to the back of the car, hoping to follow the trail of footsteps as they approached. One fairly clear print showed. Otherwise, the vandal had stayed to the side of the driveway, walking in the tall grass. The print was generic—large for a woman, perhaps, but medium for a man—smooth on the bottom with no distinguishable tread. I followed the drive to the dirt road. Here, there was an abundance of tracks.

Unfortunately, they blurred together. A tire print showed clearly that a vehicle had parked at the entrance to Mary's drive. A good imprint, about two feet long, showed in the mud beside the road. After that, the road was graveled well enough to conceal prints.

"Charlie!" Drake's voice drifted through the trees.

I walked back down the drive to my sadly smelly vehicle. Drake was beside it, peering into the woods in all directions.

"Here I am," I answered.

"I'm afraid I'll not make a good investigator," he confessed. "I just realized that I've already walked all around the car."

"It's okay," I told him. "There are other prints up by the road. Although I'm not sure we're going to learn anything from them."

"Mary phoned Steve Bradley," he told me. "I got on the line and told him to send out a service truck. It may be an hour or so before they can get out here."

I flopped down heavily on the front steps. A rather disappointing ending to a perfect weekend.

"Why don't you two come in and have breakfast, anyway," Mary invited through the screen door.

Drake nudged me. Might as well.

"Oh, Mary. Do you have anything we might use to block off a section of the roadside? Just to be sure no one drives over that tire print out there?" I asked.

She came out and we rummaged through a storage shed at the back of the property. Finally we came up with a couple of bright red five-gallon buckets. I carried them out to the road, and set one at either end of the tire print. I put a couple of large rocks in each so they wouldn't tip over. Maybe we could preserve what little evidence we had.

Breakfast was a quiet affair. So many thoughts raced through my head that I wasn't much of a conversationalist. Drake had seen me this way before, on the case we handled together in Hawaii.

He kept my coffee mug filled, and let me work out the thoughts on my own.

"I can't believe this was a random act of vandalism," I finally told him. "Our car isn't visible from the road. It seems unlikely that anyone driving around looking for trouble would just happen to pick this spot."

"So who's after us?" he said, completing my thought.

Exactly. Who knows we're in town? I could think of half a dozen off hand. More importantly, whom have we gotten close to? Who has something to fear from us?

A squeak of brakes and a revving engine signalled the approach of Steve Bradley. Drake, Mary, and I all rushed out to the front porch. The chief slowly withdrew himself from his four wheel drive patrol vehicle. A shorter man wearing a blue workshirt and pants got out of the passenger seat. He reached into the back seat and brought out a toolbox.

"Hey, Mary," Bradley drawled. "What's going on?"

Mary was still shaken by the idea that someone had come so close to her home out here in the woods. Someone with ill intent. She explained the situation quickly to Steve in a series of rambling sentences and jerky hand gestures.

"This here's Manuel from the garage in town," Steve said to Drake. "He brought that fuel line you asked for. Now, I guess we better see what we've got here. Have you all been walking around the Jeep?"

"Yeah," Drake admitted. "I'm afraid I did that."

"There are other prints," I told him. "I'll show you."

He followed me up the drive, both of us staying on the graveled parts until we came to the few footprints and the tire print at the road. Drake and Manuel turned to the Jeep's open hood.

"Maybe you can take a mold of the tire," I suggested.

"That won't be necessary," he informed me. "I recognize it. It's a Goodyear. Most popular tire they make. Probably a third of all the cars in town have this tire."

I knew without asking that the footprints would be of no use either. They were just too plain. My spirits slumped.

"Tell you what," he said. "I'll file a report anyway. You never know. And I can drive up the road and talk to the other residents. Maybe one of them came in late and saw someone parked here."

I perked up somewhat. Sure, in a town this size everyone would know the local vehicles. If one of the other residents had seen a car here, there was probably a very good chance we could find out who it was. Walking back toward the house, I felt better than I had all morning.

"We'll have to get back to Albuquerque today," I told Bradley. "Could I call you later in the week to see what you find out?"

"Sure." His tone told me not to count on much.

Manuel tossed wrenches back into his toolbox and Drake dropped the hood of the Jeep into place as I approached. I asked Manuel how much I owed him, went through a little back-and-forth as I argued that he wasn't charging enough, then went inside for my purse. I gave him twenty more than he asked for—for his time, I told him—and we watched the two men drive away in the police cruiser.

"Maybe I ought to let the dogs sleep out on the front porch from now on," Mary said. "I can't believe they didn't alert me."

"Don't be too hard on them," Drake said. "Remember, there was lots of thunder last night. Easy for someone to cover any noise they might make."

"Besides," I added, "I don't think the vandal was after you, Mary. They got what they came for. They meant to scare us off."

17

Few clouds from the previous night remained. The moist brown earth of the mountains gave way to dry dusty powder as we left the valley. By the time we reached Albuquerque the temperature had become oppressive. Matching my mood.

Laying out money for a new fuel line hadn't been on my agenda for the weekend, and the idea that someone meant to harm us left a sour taste in my mouth. Butting heads with the untalkative populace of Valle Escondido hadn't helped either. These thoughts had roiled around in my head for the past hour, and I felt ready for something physical. Usually I take out these unsettled, half aggressive, feelings by cleaning the house. But with Drake here, that seemed rude. Worrying about being rude was also eating at me. I can only keep smiling just so long.

"You okay?" He'd been watching me for a few minutes.

"Yeah." I smiled but it felt tight.

We were almost home. Maybe I'd go ahead and run the duster over things, even if it did seem rude. I needed it. Drake carried the duffle inside. Rusty loped around the backyard, thrilled at being back in his own territory. He sniffed all the corners of the yard, then rushed to the middle of the lawn and rolled, rubbing his nose and his spine on the rough surface.

I watched from the kitchen window. Drake came up behind me and put his arms around my waist.

"I get the feeling you'd like to be alone for awhile," he said.

I hadn't wanted to be that transparent. Obviously, I was.

"Do we need anything from the grocery?" he asked. "I could go. Stock us up on milk or steaks or double chocolate fudge brownies . . ."

He really was a sweetheart.

"Okay. Let's check." We looked through the refrigerator and cabinets, making a short list.

"Are you sure you don't mind?" Already I was feeling like I'd kicked him out.

"Not a bit," he assured me.

He sounded sincere.

The Jeep backed out the driveway, leaving me feeling somehow even emptier inside. Tears pricked at my eyelids. Why? Why was I becoming such an emotional wreck recently? This wasn't like me. I stomped away from the window and found my feather duster.

Thirty minutes later, the house looked better and so did I. My senses were at least on a more even keel. I pulled out the vacuum cleaner and went over the rugs in the living and dining rooms. When that was done I was breathing hard, but I felt good.

Drake had been gone almost an hour. I found myself standing by the window, watching the street. I hoped he hadn't become lost. Did he even know where the grocery store was? I probably should have thought about that. Oh well, he's a big boy. He'd figure it out.

Rusty was anxiously waiting at the back door, so I let him in. I heard the front door at the same time. See.

"Hi, honey, I'm home," he called out, coming into the kitchen. "Sorry. I just wanted to try that out for size. Couldn't resist."

I was touched, but managed to cover my tangled emotions by taking the grocery bags from him.

"Feeling better?" he asked. He came to me and cupped the side of my face with his smooth hand. "I was worried about you, sweetheart." Those stinging eyes again.

"I'm fine," I assured him. I really was, although I couldn't figure out why my eyes reacted so strongly.

He pulled me into his arms and held me there silently for a long time. My body reacted by settling into him comfortably.

"I really better check in at the office," I told him, pulling reluctantly away. "Do you mind if we run over there?"

"Are you sure you want me tagging along? You might be getting tired of having this big old stone around your neck all the time."

I assured him that he was no stone. He could come along or stay home, as he wished.

"I'll call first," I told him. "Maybe I won't even need to go in."

Sally's first words were, "When are you bringing Drake to meet me?"

She then proceeded to tell me how much mail had piled up, and how I really did need to take care of a couple of phone calls.

"Do you want to go with me?" I asked Drake as soon as I'd hung up. "Sally really is antsy to meet you."

We called Rusty in, locked the doors, and the three of us piled back into the Jeep. Ten minutes later we were pulling into the small parking area behind the office. It was mid-afternoon already. Obviously, Sally had stayed late just for this occasion.

"Hey, Drake, how's it going?" Ron poured coffee into his mug as he greeted us in the kitchen.

"Great. You been out shooting again recently?"

Sally's keen ear had picked up their voices. She came through the swinging door with a funny look on her face. Curious or coquettish, I couldn't tell. I did the introductions quickly.

"So, you want to come out to the range again?" Ron interrupted any chance Sally might have had to speak to Drake.

The men's conversation turned toward guns once more, that curious other language that I was only beginning to understand a little.

"What messages do I have?" I asked Sally, steering her out of the kitchen.

We walked to the front reception area to her desk. She took her seat and handed me a couple of pink message slips.

"Sally, how did you know Ross was the man you wanted to marry?" I asked. I tried to make the question nonchalant, but didn't pull it off.

"Ah ha," she grinned, pointing her index finger at me. "I knew it, I knew it. He's the one, isn't he?"

"Sally, spare me the giggles. I'm serious. How do you know?"

"Well, when I met Ross I was only eighteen years old. I didn't know anything. I suppose I just got lucky."

"That's not much help," I told her.

"Sorry. I don't really know what to tell you, Charlie."

"That's okay." I turned my attention to the phone messages.

My feet dragged up the stairs as I faced the prospects of what my desk probably looked like.

Actually, it wasn't bad. Settled into my chair, I managed to reduce it to three or four significant pieces by tossing all the catalogs, advertisements, and hot offers into the trash. I'm not a good bet for the junk mail people.

Of the two phone calls, one was from my friend, Linda Casper, calling to confirm our regular every-other-Wednesday lunch. I left a message with her receptionist that I'd be there.

After seeing Drake off at the airport early Wednesday morning, I had a feeling I'd be wanting companionship. Besides, Dr.

Linda might just offer some valuable insights into the case in Valle Escondido, considering that I hadn't gotten any information at all from the doctors up there.

The second call, too, was easily handled. A former client wanted a copy of her billing for tax purposes. I told her I didn't think she could deduct our charges, but agreed to send her the billing anyway. She could work that out for herself.

Male voices trailed across the hall now, telling me that Drake and Ron had settled into Ron's office. I stood in the doorway. The talk was still about guns. I wandered back to my own office.

"Those two really hit it off, didn't they?" Sally leaned against the doorjamb.

"I'll say," I motioned her to come in. "I need some input about the people in Valle Escondido, Sally. You grew up there. Give me some insight."

"Like what?" She looked genuinely puzzled.

"Oh, I don't know." I realized the question was rather general. "I just feel like I'm talking to brick walls with those people. Like I'm not seeing into them."

"In what way?"

Again, I couldn't really put my finger on it. There was some key to the mentality of that town, some underlying current that I had felt but hadn't quite stepped into. I couldn't really explain it to Sally. Instead, I told her about the slashed fuel line.

"Wow, you've stepped on somebody's toes," she said, her eyes wide.

"No kidding. But whose? That's what I mean about not being able to figure out those people. I can't think of anyone I've pissed off that much."

She stared at a spot on the far wall. Obviously, she didn't have an answer for that one, either.

"I like Drake, by the way," she whispered.

The two male voices hadn't slowed a bit across the hall.

"How can you tell?" I chided. "You met him for two minutes."

"I just know," she said wisely. "One can tell these things. He has an inner sensitivity, gentleness, kindness." Her eyes took on a faraway look.

"Oh, you." I tossed one of the trashed catalogs at her.

She jumped out of her mystical persona and giggled. "I'm going home now, if that's okay," she said. It was, after all, more than three hours past her normal quitting time. I waved vacantly as she departed.

How did she know about Drake? Sally was periodically into the study of mystical things, but I had always attributed her "visions" to PMS or something else more logical. I had to admit, though, that she had always been more attuned to nature and feelings. I tend to want numbers, answers. Spell it out for me in cold hard statistics.

Maybe I needed to tune into my spiritual side more often. Maybe therein lie the answers to the Valle Escondido mystery, and to my feelings about Drake.

18

Pop! Pop pop pop! The shots sounded like firecrackers blowing up in quick sequence. I stared at the target, my vision blurring, then clearing again. Ron had put his first three right in the bullseye.

Back to my own target. My arms were beginning to shake. My vision became clear, as I gently opened both eyes. I relaxed my arms for a minute, flexing and rolling my shoulders to work out the cramping.

One more time. Raise the pistol. Take a deep breath. Line up the sights. Let the breath out slowly. Pause. Squeeze trigger. My shot was low and to the right. Squeeze, don't pull, I reminded myself.

At least this was systematic. There was a goal; there was a logical way to that goal. None of the mystical hocus pocus that had nagged at me since talking with Sally. All yesterday afternoon and evening the vagueness of it had bothered me, like a slight headache that wouldn't go away. I was glad we had come to the range. I found the intense concentration good for me.

Today was Drake's last day here. Tomorrow morning I would drive him to the airport. He would be hundreds of miles away before I reached the office. Already something felt missing from my life. I didn't want to let myself think about it. I just wanted to shoot a bullseye before the morning was over.

Ron had brought two pistols with us. We took turns using them, the third person standing by to retrieve the brass casings, which Ron would take home and reload. A system that worked well. By noon, each of us had shot a couple hundred rounds. My improvement was beginning to show. Both men had a new admiration for the girl who had taken up a man's sport.

We lunched at McDonald's, chewing down Big Macs like hungry wolves. After the first ravages of hunger were quelled, we slowed down and talked. Drake held my hand under the table.

We had brought two cars since Ron had to rush home to shower and change before giving a deposition at three.

"Do you need to go back to the office today?" Drake asked.

I couldn't think of anything pressing, so we went home, let Rusty out in the back yard, and made love. It felt decadent, being in bed at four in the afternoon.

"What's going to happen to us, Charlie?"

He asked the question that I hadn't had the courage to face.

"Will I go back to Hawaii and never see you again?"

I lay there, cuddled against his shoulder, realizing that would be impossible. He had become too much a part of my life. We had spent seven days together, inseparable, and loving it. Having my own best friend to share with, to bounce ideas off of, to crawl into bed with. How could I simply let this go?

How could I move to Hawaii, abandoning everything familiar to me? My family, my business, my childhood friends were all here in New Mexico.

"We'll work something out," I said, kissing him lightly on the shoulder. "Even the stickiest problems have answers."

Pedro's enchiladas were especially good that night. The margaritas had just the right tang, the salt just the right bite. Colors seemed more vivid, Drake's face more handsome. I wanted to preserve it all. The morning came much too quickly.

I wanted the airport scene to blur and pass just as quickly but it didn't.

Every detail stood out, especially the unhappiness on Drake's face. I still hadn't committed to anything.

"At least promise you'll come visit me again," he asked as we stood in the departure lounge, watching his plane roll into place against the jetway. He held my hand lightly, staring at my fingers as if to memorize them.

That much I could promise, and I did.

"This isn't a very sophisticated thing for a forty year old man to say," he began, "but I'll be miserable without you."

My damn eyes reddened again. I squeezed his hand and nodded.

"Maybe I can arrange to come in September," I told him.

"It's going to be a long two months. I love you, Charlie."

"I love you, too."

A voice intruded: "Final boarding call for flight 26 . . ."

We kissed—then he was gone. Taking a great big piece of me with him.

Traffic on the freeway was medium heavy as I headed toward Linda Casper's office in the valley. Linda was in my class in high school, a serious student when most of us were preoccupied with where we could get our hands on some beer and where the next party was. She actually memorized those passages from Shakespeare that I found deadly dull. She was one of those rare students who seemed to know what she wanted from life right from the start, and she set out to have it. When my parents were killed, our junior year, Linda was one of the few who seemed to know what to say to me.

We continued this friendship in college because I settled down a bit then myself after the first two years. I realized that I was about to come into my inheritance when I turned twenty-one, and that I couldn't even balance a checkbook. An accounting course led to a real interest in numbers and finance. While our friends were still on the path to beer parties, Linda and I were coaching each other on anatomy charts and balance sheets. Now I do her taxes for her and she tries to keep me healthy. We hadn't seen each other in almost a year, until a couple of months ago when I needed stitches removed from my head. A regular Wednesday lunch plan had evolved.

The waiting room held an assortment of people, most looking bored in wood framed chairs upholstered in beige tweed. The receptionist's chair was empty, and I took the chance to peek at the sign-in sheet. It looked like Linda's last patient had arrived over an hour ago. Undoubtedly he was gone by now. The people sitting around must be waiting for Linda's associate.

"May I help you?" The voice was almost cold, as she caught me snooping. I looked up.

"Oh hi, Charlie." She warmed up when she recognized me. "Linda's almost ready, I think. Want me to check?"

"Don't disturb her," I answered. "I can wait until she's free."

"I'll tell her you're here." Her pale green uniform disappeared down the hall.

Minutes later Linda emerged. In a flowing print dress, cut well enough to conceal the chunkiness of her ample body, she didn't look quite the same without the authority of her white lab coat. Her infectious grin was the same, though, as were the short blond curls, bright blue eyes, and faint freckles under her makeup. She greeted me with a hug.

After some discussion as to whose car we'd take and where we'd eat, we were on our way to The Cooperage. Once there, I figured I could opt for either comfort food such as prime rib, or sensible food such as a salad. After my indulgences of the past week, I knew which it should be. We were lucky to get a table right away, and fifteen minutes later I carried my salad-laden plate to our table.

"So, the fabulous Drake Langston has come and gone," Linda said, setting her salad plate down and squeezing into her chair.

I sighed.

"When do I get to meet him?"

When, indeed. "I don't know, Linda. I'm trying so hard to take this one step at a time. He's talking commitment, moving in together, *marriage*. Scares the hell out of me."

"Well, if you're unsure of your feelings for him, just say no."

"Unfortunately, that's just it. I'm falling in love with him. He's kind and considerate, wonderful in bed, and he does dishes. I mean, what more could I want?"

"So, just say yes."

I put down my fork. "You're just too damn sensible, Linda." We both laughed. "I know he won't wait forever for an answer, and I know a long-distance relationship will be hard to keep going indefinitely. I'm going to have to give it some serious thought."

I speared a chunk of lettuce and swabbed it around in low-cal Ranch dressing. "Linda, could I pick your brain, professionally?"

"Sure, anytime," she replied, chewing.

"I was up in Valle Escondido last weekend, that little town north of Santa Fe? Anyway, I met a friend of Sally's who'd had a miscarriage within the last year. A friend of hers had had two. Scary thing is, the friend died from the second one. What are the odds of that?"

"Dying from a miscarriage? It happens. Not often anymore. Didn't she get prompt medical treatment?"

"Oh, yes. She'd been to her doctor that morning, and once she started hemorrhaging, they rushed her right back. It just seems curious to me that here are these two women, friends, living in the same town, and both have miscarried. That seems odd."

"Depends. Somewhere around half of all first pregnancies end in miscarriage," she said. "Thirty percent or so of second pregnancies, same thing."

"Really? That seems high."

"Lots of factors can be involved. Smoking and drinking are probably two of the biggest, but there could be environmental factors — any number of things."

I pondered all that. "I guess it just has Sally really freaked because, you know, she's pregnant. She tried so hard to get that way, it would really devastate her to lose that baby. Laura, that's Sally's friend in Valle Escondido, thinks that Cynthia's husband beat her."

"Well, that could certainly be a big environmental factor," Linda agreed. "Even stress, lifestyle, pushing herself too hard."

I thought of Cynthia's job, with Barbara Lewis breathing down her neck constantly.

"Oh, gosh, look at the time." Linda looked at her watch. "We better hustle a bit. I've got an appointment at one."

We finished our salads quickly and I drove her back to the office. We agreed to meet again the following Wednesday.

Back at the office, I found myself unable to settle into work, although I had plenty of it waiting for me. Where was Drake right now? He should have reached Flagstaff and would be visiting with his mother. What were they talking about? Suddenly, I wanted to meet her.

Sally had gone for the day, which was just as well. Linda's revelations were still fresh in my head and I didn't want to alarm Sally by getting onto the subject of miscarriages. I was shuffling papers around on my desk, looking busy but finding no focus whatsoever when Ron walked in.

"So, he's on his way, huh?" Ron asked.

"Yeah. Should be at his mother's by now." I could hear the flatness in my own voice.

"I really like Drake. Think he might become a permanent fixture around here?" His tone was playful.

"I don't know, Ron, I just don't know." I slapped an envelope down on my desk. "I just wish everyone would quit pressuring me about this."

I pushed past him and slammed the bathroom door. My shaky hands pressed hard against the cool porcelain sink. Tears welled, then rolled down my cheeks. My insides quivered like jelly. In the mirror, a miserable reddened face stared back at me. I missed him so much.

What was happening to me? I'd never felt so happy around a man or so miserable when we were apart. It was so unlike me to base my own happiness on another person. Is this what love feels like? I took a deep breath.

I splashed cold water on my face, used the potty, and went out to face Ron. He was seated meekly at his desk.

"I'm sorry, Ron. You didn't deserve that." My lower lip quivered as I said it.

He stood and circled the desk to put his arms around me. Made some there-there noises but refrained from any comment that might get his head bitten off again. Finally, I sniffed deeply and looked up at him.

"It's confusing, huh?" He was probably referring to the disastrous love affair he'd recently recovered from.

I nodded, feeling the slight sense of relief that a good cry can bring. I flopped into the chair opposite his desk.

"Hey, you'll figure it out," he said, returning to his own chair.

"He wants me to move to Hawaii," I whined.

"Life in paradise? Anybody I know would jump at the chance."

"So why am I not jumping? What about the office, our business, all my friends? What about the house I've lived in since the day I was born? How could I leave all that?"

"Scared to think about leaving? Or scared of a committed relationship?"

"That's exactly what I've been asking myself." I blew out a deep breath. "Well, I've got time. I'll work it out, like you said."

The phone rang, startling us both. Ron picked it up, answering in his usual gruff tone. Listened a minute. "For you," he said, punching the hold button.

I rose from the chair. "I'll go to my office so you can get back to your work."

"Charlie? Steve Bradley, in Valle Escondido here."

"Yes, Steve, how are things there?"

"Well, I thought I'd update you on the fuel line incident."

"You found some witnesses?"

"Nothing too helpful, I'm afraid. One neighbor on that road said they were coming home late that night and noticed a vehicle stopped along the side. Only thing is, it was raining so hard they really didn't get a good look. They described it as big and dark."

A big dark vehicle. "No plate numbers? They didn't recognize it as local?"

"Just big and dark. This is a little old lady who isn't exactly up on all the latest car models. You could probably stand her in front of the car in broad daylight with the license plates and brand name showing, and she'd still describe it as 'big and dark'."

"No other witnesses, I suppose." Not really daring to hope at this point. "What about any new developments in the Cynthia Martinez case?"

"What Cynthia Martinez case, Charlie?" he was beginning to sound impatient. "We have no evidence that hers wasn't a simple medical complication of pregnancy. There is no case."

"Okay." I agreed with him for the sake of maintaining civility but I was not convinced, by far. If there was nothing suspicious about Cynthia's death, why did my asking a few questions around town bring about vandalism to my car? There was no doubt in my mind that the incident was a warning. No doubt at all.

I made a few more polite noises to Bradley, ending the conversation on a 'have a nice day' kind of note. My fingers were doing a drum-roll on the desktop. My mind danced from Valle Escondido to Drake to the stack of billing that awaited my attention. I couldn't seem to settle on a topic.

"You aren't by any chance looking for something to do?" Ron interrupted my mental free-fall.

"Hmm? Oh, well, whatever." I indicated the stacks of papers I should be working on.

"If you're busy, it's okay," he assured me, "but I need some research done and . . . you're so much better at it than I am."

I flashed him a skeptical look.

"I'm doing a report for the state investigators newsletter. On missing persons cases. I just need some data. I think you can get it at the main library."

"Sure, I'd be glad to," I said, standing up and reaching for my purse.

"You would?"

"Why not? I'm not accomplishing anything here but moping around. I might as well be doing something constructive."

"Okay, here's the information I need." He handed me a slip of paper with some notes in his scritchy writing.

I neatened a couple of piles of paper on my desk and switched off the light.

"I'll probably go straight home after I'm finished," I told him, "unless you need this stuff tonight."

"No, tomorrow's fine. And Charlie? Thanks."

I lowered all the windows in the Jeep, letting the stuffy hot air out. It was our thirty-fifth day without rain and the heat waves rose off the streets as I made my way east. All the traffic in the downtown area seemed outbound. I had no trouble finding a parking spot next to the library. The small parking lot was ringed by young trees and I was lucky enough to get a space where a little late afternoon shade would cover my car. I thought longingly of the cool afternoon air at Mary McDonald's house in the mountains.

Air conditioning in the library provided a welcome contrast to the outside air. I found myself a computer terminal and logged on to the subject index. New Mexico statistics by county. M-I-S-brought up a listing where I should find missing persons information.

Miscarriages

Misdemeanors

Missing Persons

Here was Ron's topic, but curiosity wasn't going to let me pass up the other, more timely one. I jotted down the reference location where I'd find it and headed into the stacks. The most recent information was for the previous year but it was a good start.

Miscarriages. By county. DeBaca, Dona Ana, Eddy, Escondido. Within each county, the stats were broken down by various factors, including the mother's age, race, blood type, and other factors such as smoking, drinking, drug use and so on. My finger trailed down the page to Escondido County. In Escondido County, the number of miscarriages were significantly higher per capita than for all other counties. I went back to the preceding county listings. Why in Escondido County?

Was there some environmental factor there that didn't pertain to the rest of the state? It didn't make much sense. I slipped the book back onto the shelf.

Remembering my real errand here, I looked up the references for missing persons cases. I didn't know Ron's real purpose in his report, so I carried the book to the copier, fed dimes into it, and copied all pages I felt might be useful.

Five o'clock. Outside, the heat felt worse than ever, like all the go-home traffic had caused a ten degree jump in the air temperature. The small speckling of shade across my Jeep hadn't made any great difference; it was still like an oven inside. I tossed the papers onto the passenger seat beside me, rolled all windows down and let the car idle until the blast of heat from the air conditioner subsided a little.

Rusty had been home alone all day I realized, feeling a bit guilty for ignoring him. I joined the traffic flow west on Central, eager to get home where I could strip down to shorts, pull my stiflingly warm hair up off my neck, and find some iced tea. And after that? I mentally composed little tasks I could do to keep the time from dragging and the emptiness of the bedroom from getting to me.

He greeted me at the door, that red-brown bundle of energy, and after licking my hands and sniffing to see if I'd brought home any food, Rusty turned to the door expectantly checking to see if Drake were behind me. I felt my throat tighten.

"Sorry, boy, he's not here anymore."

Rusty glanced out through the screen once again, just to be sure. I went straight to the bedroom to change into cooler clothing.

The empty bed, with rumpled sheets and coverlet spilling over the edges, faced me. I sprawled on it face down, burying my nose in Drake's pillow, breathing in the scent of him. Loneliness was an emotion I'd never experienced before and I didn't like it a bit.

Rusty's nails clicked across the hardwood floor and I felt him sniffing my outstretched leg. I rolled to my side and reached a hand toward him. His large sad eyes mirrored my own.

"Come on, you," I scolded. "We can't go around like this all day. I'm going to change my clothes and we'll have some dinner."

Words pertaining to food are tops in this dog's vocabulary and the reaction was immediate. He danced around me as I smoothed the sheets and made the bed. I carried a few stray dirty clothes to the hamper in the bathroom, pulled my hair into a pony tail with a stretchy cloth band, and shed the slacks and cotton sweater I'd worn all day in favor of shorts and a T-shirt.

I opened the back door for Rusty. While he sniffed out his favorite corner of the yard, I scooped some nuggets into his bowl then poured myself a big iced tea. The back yard was pleasantly shady so I carried his bowl and my glass out to the patio. He set right to it while I flipped through the mail I'd brought in with me. A few bills to pay would give me something to do this evening.

A noise on my right caught my attention.

"Hi, Charlie." Elsa Higgins' face peeked tentatively through the hedge.

"Gram! Hi, come on over."

I watched her negotiate the worn path between our two properties. She was looking a little older and more frail every time I saw her. At eighty-six, she's still pretty feisty, though. She lives alone, cleans her own house, and plants a garden every summer. When my parents died, my junior year in high school, she took me into her home until I was old enough to be on my own. She saved my ass a few times, while I probably gave her a lot of her white hair.

"Your beau gone already?" she asked.

I smiled at the old-fashioned word. "Yes, I took him to the airport this morning."

"I sure like him," she confided. "He's a real hunk."

Now I had to laugh out loud. "Yes, Gram, I guess you could say he's a hunk."

We sat quietly on the padded patio chairs not speaking for awhile.

"I knew he was special when you first came back from Hawaii," she said. "It just showed on your face."

It seemed everyone I knew was convinced that Drake was the right man for me. They just didn't have to deal with the distance problem.

"Have you had any dinner yet, Charlie?"

"No, but I had a big lunch," I told her.

"I have some sliced cold turkey. I could make us a sandwich," she suggested.

I still didn't feel any immediate hunger pangs, but thought about her. Old people sometimes don't eat the way they should because they don't have anyone to eat with. And I got the feeling she was offering the sandwich as an excuse for some companionship.

"Sure, let's do it," I agreed. "I'll come help you put them together."

We stepped off the porch and walked toward her kitchen door, Rusty trotting behind. Her house was stuffy-hot and smelled of burnt toast. The contrast with the outside air made it all the more noticeable.

"I guess I never turned on the air-conditioning today," she remarked.

"Gram, it was ninety-five degrees out! How could you stand it?"

"I guess I'm just getting cold-blooded," she answered. "Switch it on if you want."

"Well, you might sleep better tonight if the house is a little cooler." I located the thermostat switch in the living room and turned it on. I'd have to remember to switch it off when I left or she'd get too chilled.

Together we made the sandwiches and I suggested that we carry them out to the patio to eat. The sun was low now, casting long shadows in the gold-tinted yard. Gram began telling me about her garden and rambled into stories from her childhood with only an occasional acknowledgement from me. I made attentive noises and found my mind wandering back to the statistics I'd read this afternoon at the library. Perhaps I'd suggest that Sally and I take another drive up to Valle Escondido in the next few days.

19

The tires hummed as the scenery flew by. Grass, parched tan by the long dry spell, waved along the roadside interspersed with dust-covered pinon trees. Yesterday, Sally and I had planned this Friday trip but she didn't feel well this morning and I didn't especially want to be taking care of a puking preggie the whole time. On a whim I decided to make the trip back to Valle Escondido by myself.

Low clouds hung on the horizon, obscuring the mountaintops as I approached Santa Fe. The air had cooled considerably and the dimness was easy on the eyes. We might just be in for some rain, finally.

I passed the turnoffs to Santa Fe, staying with I-25 on a path that was becoming routine. I thought of Mary McDonald's bed and breakfast in the mountains north of Valle Escondido. Now that would be a pleasant place to live. I wondered what Drake would think about relocating to the mainland and becoming a mountain person once again. I stopped myself, knowing that I was coming dangerously close to making plans.

I approached the little town with a familiarity that grew with each visit. A bright blue mini-van that I'd noticed on the Ford dealer's lot had been sold. The drive-in had replaced some burned out light bulbs. I realized that this was my third trip here in less than two weeks.

At the bank, the parking lot was full. Friday. I pulled in, thinking perhaps Laura would be available for lunch. I might get an update on the aftermath of Cynthia's passing before I approached anyone else in town. I still wasn't exactly sure what I hoped to find—I had some vague idea of following up on the statistics I'd read about.

Laura was behind her teller window with a long line of customers facing her. Her short hairstyle and dark blue suit made her look businesslike and efficient. She wore a red patterned scarf at the throat and had a gold swirl of a pin on her jacket lapel. I joined the customer line, waiting my turn to speak with her. She spotted me when I was still third in line. Knowing I didn't have bank business, she waved me to the front. Several sets of eyes bored into my back.

"Hi, Charlie," she greeted enthusiastically.

"Do you have a lunch break soon?" I asked.

"Ten minutes."

"I'll wait outside. I need to talk to you." I told her.

The sun was trying valiantly to come through the clouds as an upper wind moved them briskly along. Tired petunias drooped in a concrete planter beside the walkway. I perched on the edge of it, watching the traffic as I waited for Laura. She came along sooner than I expected.

"Where's a good place for lunch, where we can talk privately?" I asked.

"Oh, anyplace," she said. "Rosa's?"

We took my Jeep and were soon settled at a corner table that offered some degree of seclusion. The preliminary rituals of placing our order and getting iced tea delivered to the table took only a few minutes.

"Well, is anything new going on around here?" I asked.

"Haven't heard a thing. Cynthia's name is very carefully avoided around the bank. Richard was out of town for a couple of days—I haven't heard where."

"I was at the library in Albuquerque recently and I read some unusual statistics," I told her. "Maybe you can help me with this."

Our waitress arrived with steaming plates of enchiladas just then and we paused conversation long enough to watch her set them down using potholders. She asked if everything was okay and I assumed she meant at the table, since I doubted she wanted to hear our entire life stories.

"Laura, can you give me the names of anyone else you can think of who's had a miscarriage in the past year or two?" I pulled out a pen and jotted names on my paper napkin.

"Well, Cynthia, of course. Um, let's see." She chewed on her lower lip. "A woman my sister works with . . . Pauline . . . Pauline Baca. And, um, Rosemary Garcia. She lives down the street from me. And, well, you know that I did—well two times actually, but the first one was about four years ago."

I took a bite of cheese enchilada dripping with green chile sauce. Laura was still thinking. I didn't want to interrupt her thoughts. She gave a couple more names.

"And did all the women go to the doctors here in town?" I asked.

"I'm pretty sure they did," she said, wiping her mouth. "Although there are some people here who'll drive to Santa Fe for medical treatment. Well, our clinic is so small, you know."

"Who was your doctor?"

"Dr. Phillips. Evan Phillips."

"He's the older of the two brothers, isn't he?" I asked.

"Yes, I feel a little funny going to Rodney Phillips, since we were in the same class in school. I mean, not for a cold or that kind of thing, but . . . you know."

Female stuff. I really couldn't blame her.

"Rodney treats mostly older patients. He's really good with them. And the new one, Doctor Fisher, he mostly sees kids. He's new here, I mean, didn't grow up here."

"How long has he been in town?"

"Oh, probably two or three years. Everybody seems to like him. He always has a smile for you when you go in."

"Is there a domestic violence facility here?" I asked. "Not that all these miscarriages were caused that way," I hastened to add. From observing them, I felt sure that Laura's husband Bobby was a kind and gentle man.

She looked upward, thinking. "I think a group meets a few times a week at the church. You could check the classified ads in the local paper. They run a little listing there."

Our waitress refilled our tea glasses and tucked the check between the salt and pepper shakers. Rosa's enchiladas were as wonderful as before, but I had to admit I was feeling stuffed.

"Did your doctor give any explanation for your two miscarriages, Laura?"

She shrugged, her face becoming a little tight. "Just that these things happen sometimes."

"I sure would like to talk to the doctors about all this." Even as I said it, I knew the chances of getting any real information were slim. No doctor in today's litigious environment would give out patient information, especially to a stranger.

Laura nodded agreement but didn't give any suggestions as to how I might get them talking.

"Maybe I'll drop in on Richard Martinez, too," I mused. I still wasn't convinced that he didn't have something to do with Cynthia's death.

I dropped Laura off at the bank and stopped at a convenience store to buy the latest issue of the *Valle Gazette*. It was a small weekly paper, slightly bigger than tabloid size. Page four carried a brief mention of the Martinez funeral without commenting on the outburst Richard had directed toward Barbara Lewis. I skimmed it before flipping to the classifieds. The ad read:

Does your partner threaten, belittle, or hit you? Get help in a confidential, caring atmosphere. Meetings M-W-F eves 7:00 Community Center.

There was a number to call for more information. I didn't think I'd learn anything much different at this group than the one I'd attended in Albuquerque, but it might be interesting to see who else was there.

Meanwhile, the clouds had thickened and the wind whipped tree tops into swirling tangles of green. Dust snaked up the main street, sidewinding until it hit the curbs. Bits of trash and dried weed pieces spiralled upward in a traveling dust devil. I powered up all the windows on my Jeep and waited it out.

I thought about talking to Richard Martinez once again, but wasn't sure what I'd say to him. He hadn't exactly been open with me when I'd visited his home before. Jennifer Lang had pretty well filled me in on Cynthia's movements on the day of her death. Besides, I was a little uneasy about being alone with Richard. There was still something about the man I didn't trust.

I started the Jeep and began driving.

Without planning, I found myself on the north edge of town where I seemed to be watching for the turnoff to Mary McDonald's place. The wind was hardly a breeze here as I wound my way farther down the dirt lane between steep hills. The summer flowers raised their heads as if hoping for a cool shower from the sky. The cloud of dust from my tires settled on them as I passed. I slowed sympathetically.

Mary stood in her yard, aiming a hose at the planter boxes beside the porch railing. She stared, squinting at my vehicle as I pulled into the drive, then broke into a smile when she realized who it was. She shifted the hose to a different planter as I got out of the car.

"Hey, Charlie," she greeted, "where's the rest of your bunch?"

"Well, Drake is on his way back to Hawaii," I sighed. "I left Rusty home with my neighbor this trip. Didn't know how long I'd be and I felt guilty about making him stay in the car a lot while I talk to people."

"Shoot, you could have brought him out here to romp with mine," she assured me.

"Next time I'll remember that."

We both stared at the spray of water as she guided the hose over the thick heads of columbine, washing the road dust off them and turning their leaves a cool green once again. She carried the hose across the meandering lawn to a winding flower bed on the other side.

"This ground is so dry, I think I'll let this just soak awhile," she said. She laid the sprayer down, aiming it downhill. At the side of the house, she adjusted the water volume to a slow trickle.

"Now," she continued, wiping her damp hands against her jeans, "let's go inside and have a lemonade."

I followed her into the kitchen while she pulled two tall glasses from the cupboard and a large pitcher from the refrigerator. "I wish I had a bed to offer you for the night, Charlie," she said, "but I've got the rooms all full up. The people ought to be here around six."

"Oh, I didn't mean to . . ."

"But anytime you're in town, I want you to check with me. If I've got an empty room, it's yours."

She handed me a full glass and we clicked them together. We each took a long sip.

"Whew," she continued. "I been out in that yard all morning and I'm ready for a break. Let's sit in the living room and put our feet up."

"Mary," I began, as we were burrowing into the deep sofa cushions, "I'm still curious about Cynthia Martinez's death. I'm not really sure why I came to you, except to find a friendly face."

"Good enough reason for me," she said.

"Well, I'm still not convinced that Richard didn't somehow cause the miscarriage. I just can't figure out how. I understand there wasn't evidence of any new injuries."

She drank again from her glass, then set it down on a coaster on the coffee table. "It's a puzzle, isn't it?"

"A couple of days ago, I was in the Albuquerque library and found some really strange statistics on miscarriages in this state. And Escondido County was by far the highest per capita."

"Really? That does seem odd."

"You've never heard this before? No investigative reporter has grabbed onto it and done stories for the newspaper?"

"Not that I've ever heard," she answered.

"I thought I might go to the domestic violence support group meeting tonight," I told her. "See if I can find any correlation between the women there and this particular health risk."

The two dogs were whining at the door so Mary got up to let them in. They trotted over to me and sniffed me carefully to be sure I belonged.

"You told me that you were friends with the older Dr. Phillips, didn't you?" I asked. "Suppose there's any chance he'd be candid with you about Cynthia's death?"

"We weren't that good of friends even in school," she said. "More like acquaintances, I'd say. Even so, I doubt Evan would tell me anything. It's not like we're social equals, you know."

"Umm." I had known that would be the answer. Even Linda Casper, with whom I was good friends, probably wouldn't open up with any details on a patient's case.

"Tell me any other women you know who've miscarried," I suggested "like within the last year or two. I'm trying to get some idea."

She stared into the cold black fireplace, thinking. "I don't know, Charlie, I can think of maybe one or two. Not being into all that pregnancy and motherhood stuff myself, I really don't keep very good track of it."

I knew what she meant. This was hardly my real area of interest either.

She gave me a couple of names, which I jotted down on the same napkin that I'd taken notes on at lunch. I thanked her for the lemonade and carried the empty glasses to the kitchen. She walked me out to the car.

"Now, you remember what I said about that room," she reminded. "I'd love to have you stay with me anytime."

I thanked her again and waved as I turned the Jeep around and headed out her driveway. Random drops of rain struck the windshield, forming mud spots with the road dust. By the time I reached the main road again, they had quit although the sky looked more threatening than ever. I thought about going to the support group meeting that evening and then driving all the way home late and in potentially bad weather. Decided to get a room at the Ponderosa Inn instead.

This being a Friday night in the summer, I figured I better get my room early, just in case they might fill up. The desk clerk greeted me unenthusiastically, giving me one sideways haven't-we-met-before glance while handing me the registration card. He mechanically recited the locations of the ice and vending machines and told me where my room was. It was only two rooms away from where Sally and I had stayed our first night here.

I parked right outside the ground-floor room and carried in my small duffle containing one change of clothes, a smattering of toiletries and the pistol Ron had insisted I bring. Plopping the bag on one of the double sized beds with its faded geometric patterned bedspread, I transferred the gun to my purse, washed my face and hands and tried to decide what to do next.

My note-napkin was becoming rather crumpled as I pulled it from my purse. I took out my small spiral notebook and transferred the names and other assorted scribbles to it. All the names Laura had given me were Hispanic women. Did that have anything to do with the miscarriage rate, or was it simply that most of her friends were of her own race? My head was beginning to hurt from the oppressive heat and the sound of the wind whistling around the cheap aluminum window frames. I stretched out on the empty bed and woke up more than an hour later.

My head felt no better but I knew I had to get moving or I'd lie there the rest of the evening. I popped two aspirin from the assorted toiletries bag and bought a canned Coke from the motel's vending machine on my way out to the car.

The Family Health Clinic was only about two blocks up the road. It was nearly five o'clock and I had no idea what their hours were, but decided there was one way to find out.

The parking lot was full when I arrived. I squeezed into a space at the side of the adobe colored stucco building just as a man and woman emerged and vacated a spot right by the front door. A black plastic sign with changeable white letters was stuck to the front glass door, announcing that the clinic closed at five on weekdays. My watch showed three minutes till, and the waiting room was just as jammed as the parking lot.

A couple of the patients looked rather impatient as I walked in, probably viewing me as competition for the doctor's remaining three minutes. I approached the beige Formica reception desk. The same receptionist, Chris Smith, was on duty, her well-made-up eyes still the best feature in her pudgy face. The short-short hair had been dressed up a bit with some curl at the top, although the small head impression was still distinct. I glued the friendliest smile I could muster onto my face.

"Hi, Chris, remember me?"

She looked a little vague, although her mouth managed to mirror my smile.

"Charlie Parker, from Albuquerque? I was here the Fourth of July." I schmoozed shamelessly. "I was back in town for the day and thought I'd stop in and say hi."

Something finally clicked in and recognition flickered in her eyes. "Oh, yeah, how are you?"

"Oh, I'm fine, but my friend Sally isn't doing too great," I said. "Cynthia Martinez's miscarriage really hit her hard. Sally's pregnant, too, you know and I guess it really worries her that the same thing could happen to her."

She did some sympathetic head nods without really having the faintest idea what I was getting at.

I dropped my voice to just above a whisper and moved closer to her. "Did they ever figure out what happened with Cynthia? I mean, I heard there was a big to-do at the funeral between her husband and her boss." My eyes grew wider and hers followed suit.

"Well," she said hesitantly, "I really don't know much about it."

"One of the girls that worked with her said the rumor around the bank was that the husband abused her. That could have caused it, don't you think?"

She glanced nervously toward the double doors leading to the back. I wondered how many of the three doctors were on the premises at the time.

"I was reading something recently that said there were more miscarriages in this county than any other in the state." I was practically whispering by now. "I'm trying to figure out how that could be."

"Chris, I need this billing totalled right away." Dr. Rodney Phillips emerged soundlessly through the swinging doors. I straightened up and pretended to be engrossed in a pamphlet on lowering your cholesterol.

Chris busied herself at her adding machine, acting like she hadn't just been leaning over the counter to catch my whispered conversation. Phillips was giving me a narrow-eyed look that plainly said he was struggling to figure out where he'd seen me before. I refused to make eye contact.

He reached absently for the form Chris handed back to him, but I could tell he was still speculating about me. He obviously didn't want to appear so uncool as to come out and ask if we'd met somewhere, but he didn't have much other excuse for hanging around the reception desk.

A nurse appeared from the back and called out a patient name. About half the population of the waiting room followed, clearing the afternoon schedule considerably. She nodded toward Dr. Phillips, indicating that they were all his. He hadn't much choice but to usher them into an inner room. I breathed normally again after he'd left.

"Look, I'm not sure what you're after," said Chris, "but I got chewed on the last time you were here and I don't think I better talk to you any more."

"Really?" I tried to make my face look completely innocent and realized I failed totally.

"Yeah, really. You know I can't give out any patient information, so please don't ask." Two worry wrinkles etched themselves between her large blue eyes, pleading.

"Look, I didn't want to get you in trouble," I assured her. "I'm just trying to help a friend. I'll go."

She was visibly relieved to see me turn away. Outside again, I started the Jeep and adjusted the air conditioner fan to high, hoping to blow out most of the hot air quickly. As I shifted into reverse, I glanced up to see two faces at one of the clinic's windows. I would have sworn they were looking out at me.

A horn behind me startled my foot to the brake pedal. The driver of the car I'd almost backed into glared at me. When I looked back toward the clinic, that window was dark. Within minutes, I decided that I'd imagined the faces.

20

Dinner. My stomach was beginning to talk, although after having enchiladas for lunch I knew I better keep it light. I located a diner-style place that advertised "American Food." Hoping that might mean something like soup or salad, I pulled in. In any other town it could have been a Denny's or a Big Boy or maybe a Perkins. Here it was called Sal's. No evidence of whether Sal was male or female.

Padded booths upholstered in bold yellow flowers lined the walls. A salad bar filled the back third of the one main room, which pretty much answered the question of what I would order, although I did give the menu a quick browse. Most everything else was fried or sauced or gravied, so I stuck with my first instinct.

"And what can I git you ta drink?" She looked like the type who had grown up and spent all her life in this same town, probably in the same diner, but the accent was West Texas. Her large blond hair reminded me of Dolly Parton's early years. In fact, her shape wasn't too unlike Dolly's either. She flashed a big genuine smile my way after taking my iced tea order and telling me to "hep yourself at the salad bar."

I loaded a plate with everything that looked crisp and cold and was, as nearly as I could remember, fat free. I carried the heaping platter back to the table, arriving in sync with my iced tea-bearing waitress.

"You just visiting for the weekend?" she asked. "Ain't seen you around before."

"I've been here a couple of times," I said. I explained that I was looking into Cynthia Martinez's death.

"That sure was a shame," she said, sympathetically. "I was just so shocked. She was just the nicest lady."

"Was she in here often?"

"Like just about ever' day at lunch," she said. "Always had a salad and a fruit juice. In the winter, she'd get hot soup, but only if it wasn't the creamy kind. She really watched those fat grams, you know. She was a healthy eater."

She left to fill another customer's coffee cup at the far end of the room. I stabbed at my salad, picking out my favorite things first.

"Yep, she really wanted that baby." She continued the conversation right where she'd left off. "She sure took good care of herself. Went to her doctor appointments real regular an' all." She refilled my iced tea, then sat down across from me. I wondered briefly whether Sal would mind.

"One of the women she worked with told me that they saw evidence that her husband abused her," I said quietly, as if whispering would make the remark seem less tactless.

She nodded, the blond curls remaining firmly in place. "I always suspected," she said wisely. "Suspected, but you know, just didn't feel it was my place . . ."

"The doctors said her hemorrhaging was a result of the miscarriage, not anything the husband did."

"Hmph. Them. I don't go to them doctors here. I go to Santa Fe to see my G-Y-N. Don't like spreadin' my legs for the same guys I serve lunch to, you know?"

She scooted her rear to the outside edge of the booth. "Looks like we got some more customers," she said, heading toward the front.

I worked my way through the rest of the salad as I watched her lead the newcomers to a booth discreetly far from mine. She quickly took their orders, filled water glasses, and turned the order in at the kitchen. The coffee drinker at the back of the room was ready to leave. He dropped a dollar bill on the table and slowly ambled toward the cash register.

" 'Night, Sal," he said, leaving his check and some cash by the register. So, I'd been talking to the boss.

I hoped she'd come back and visit some more but the dinner crowd hit in full force. Sal bustled efficiently about, the only waitress to handle all the tables. I left enough to cover the check and a fairly generous tip so she wouldn't have to break stride to make change for me.

Six-thirty. The sun was still bright, dimming only a bit as it reached toward the western hills. It would be another half-hour before the domestic violence group met, but getting there early might give me the chance to talk with the counselor on my own. Consulting a cartoon-like tourist map I'd found near Sal's cash register, I learned that the Community Center was about two blocks off Main Street near the center of town.

Fresh black paving with bright yellow parking lines surrounded the adobe style building. A massive cottonwood tree whose trunk must have been nearly four feet in diameter had been paved around, leaving the ancient giant intact. Smaller, younger trees—sycamore, ash, and cottonwood—circled the lot and the building. Chamisa and juniper shrubs nestled in against the foundation, snuggling for protection. Only a half-dozen cars dotted the lot and I parked among them, as near to the front door as I could.

The light brown building was three stories tall, towering above almost everything else in town. Blue double wooden doors, each with about a dozen glass panes, led into a small lobby. A ticket booth stood on my right, dark and empty now. A solid set of double doors stood open directly across the lobby from me, leading to a small auditorium with a stage at the front facing ascending rows of blue theater seats.

To both the left and right, hallways flanked the auditorium, presumably leading to offices and other meeting rooms. A hand lettered sign on an easel said DOMESTIC VIOLENCE GROUP, with an arrow pointing to the right. I eased my way down the hall until I came to a room whose door stood open, spilling light into the dim hallway.

A woman was in the process of creating a cozy circle of chairs, a dozen or so in number. She wore a multi-colored broomstick skirt and a tunic-length turquoise sweater. Strands of beads with various colored crystals hung around her neck, cluttering the front of the sweater. Her salt and pepper hair hung to the middle of her back, pulled away from her face by silver and turquoise combs.

"Hi," she greeted warmly. "I don't think we've met." She came toward me, hand extended.

"Charlie Parker," I said.

"First names only here," she said gently.

Right. Support group etiquette.

"I'm Mandy," she introduced. "It's good to meet you Charlie. You're a little early . . ." She glanced around at the nearly-arranged room.

"Well, I was hoping to talk to you a few minutes before everyone else arrives," I told her. "You are the group's counselor?"

"Yes. Sure, what can I help you with?" She looked ready to hear an outpouring about my mate's abusive tendencies.

"I'm not in an abusive relationship," I began. Just the opposite. "I'm really here for some research."

She stiffened just a little.

"Look, I can assure you that no names will leave here. That I won't approach anyone personally."

"What kind of research?" Her voice was firm without being cold — barely.

"Cynthia Martinez was a friend of a friend of mine," I began. I briefly outlined the situation. "I'm just wondering whether Cynthia ever came to this group."

She started to protest and I held my hand up. "I know you probably don't want to tell me that. But a woman has died under very suspicious circumstances. Her friends say she was abused. I just wonder if she was trying to get help or not."

She fidgeted from one foot to the other. Her eyes darted around the room. "Some women . . . well, some women come for awhile then feel they have everything back under control. It usually means that the man has crawled back to them, begging forgiveness, promising never to hit again, and they want to believe that he means it."

I waited while her eyes darted some more.

"Sometimes," she continued, "women believe that having a baby will make everything in the relationship all better. It rarely does, in fact usually makes everything worse, but they cling to that hope."

"And Cynthia believed that?"

She shrugged and resumed arranging the chairs. I set my bag on the floor and grabbed a couple of chairs to help.

"Have there been any other women in the group, say in the past couple of years, that have fit the same profile?" I asked.

She met my eyes with a straight-on look, a nod just barely tilting her head.

"Have any of them miscarried?"

"Some." Her answer was so soft that I barely caught it.

Voices in the hall disrupted my thoughts before I could formulate the next question. Mandy slipped to my side.

"You can stay for group," she murmured, "but don't ask any direct questions. Most of these women are really scared when they get here. Anything that makes you sound like a nosy reporter is going to send them running."

Women filed into the room, sometimes in twos and threes, but usually alone. They ranged in age from late teens to around sixty. Some were clearly friends, greeting each other with hugs and words of concern. I picked up my purse, wanting to sit at the back of the room. With the chairs in a circle, there were no invisible seats, so I braced myself for playing the role of an abused woman.

Mandy began the meeting with a few words of welcome. I gathered that most of the group had been here before, but she didn't single out anyone, namely me, as a visitor. She nodded to the woman immediately on her left, a silent cue.

"Hi, my name's Sara," the woman said, "and I live with an abusive man."

The ritual continued around the room until they came to me. My mouth went dry and my heart pounded visibly under my shirt.

"Hi, my name's Charlie . . ." I began.

21

Two hours later, I was happy to get outside into the fresh night air. Pink-gold lights illuminated the parking lot. Beyond them, a pure black sky was dotted with thousands of white pin-pricks. I breathed deeply, shaking off the tension that had built in my shoulders since the meeting started. I had behaved myself, introducing myself in the prescribed way, strange as it felt. I hadn't contributed a sad story but had listened intently to the others.

The meeting had gone very much the same way as the one I'd attended in Albuquerque, but somehow this one left me feeling depressed. In the big city, I wanted to blame the fast life for the high tension and flaring tempers that led to the women begging for help. Here, though, in a little rural town with the clean air, the tranquil pace, and the towering mountains within touching distance, I wanted to believe that such things as men beating their wives behind closed doors didn't happen. I felt deflated.

A couple of the faces looked vaguely familiar. I didn't believe I knew them, but may have seen them around town. The bank, the wake, the doctor's offices, the variety store—I couldn't say. None of the women at the meeting had been pregnant. When one mentioned her miscarriage as the turning point when her husband had hit for the first time, Mandy flashed me a tiny warning look. I was not to pursue it here.

I breathed again of the clean air before unlocking my Jeep and heading back toward the motel. There was no way I'd settle down enough to sleep for awhile yet. I stopped at a drive in and ordered french fries and a large Coke, undoing all the good I'd accomplished with my salad at dinner. The evening was warm and I sat in the car, methodically dipping each potato stick into a puddle of catsup on my serving tray, consuming them in tiny bites and savoring every greasy morsel. Indigestion would probably hit me at three a.m. but at this point I didn't care.

The brightly lit drive in, with the carhops bustling back and forth, helped distract me. Half the slots were filled with cars full of teens, boom boxes thumping, and more arriving all the time. Flirtatious girls called out to cars full of boys. If the boys looked, the girls went into fits of giggles. Some things never change. I wondered how many of these girls would be married to these boys ten years from now. And how many of them would eventually attend Mandy's group or one like it?

By ten I had run out of fries, was tempted to order more, and convinced myself that it would be a stupid thing to do. I nursed my Coke awhile longer until the people-watching became tiresome. I thought about Drake, on his way back to Kauai by now, or perhaps already there. I'd lost track of the days. I missed having him here to talk things over with. Had the feeling that I'd have really bent his ear after this evening's meeting. Was that what best friends were all about? It had been so long since I'd had one.

The cars around me had thinned out, the movies now over and the kids required to be home. Or perhaps they were simply cruising to the other end of town and back. A tiredness blanketed me and it seemed like a good time to settle into my room.

Ron's words of caution came back at me as I locked and chained the door. I pulled the pistol from my purse and stowed it under the pillow next to the one I intended to use. I switched on the TV for company, brushed my teeth and slipped out of my clothes. At home I normally sleep in nothing but panties, but here somehow, a hundred miles from home, alone in a motel, I felt vulnerable, naked. I dragged a T-shirt from my bag and tugged it on.

Late night television lulled me gently into a heavy-lidded stupor. Reaching for the remote control to switch off the glowing monitor was the last thing I remembered.

Until I became aware of movement in the room.

It took two or three seconds for me to realize where I was. A square of yellow-orange light ringed the pitch black window drapes. Strange wedges of light and shadow played on the ceiling opposite the transom. The back of the room, with the shadowy bathroom and small alcove with chrome bar that passed for a closet, were behind me. Again, I sensed more than heard movement. Nerves tingling, I felt like every hair on my body stood on end. My eyes were pasted to the door. Something wasn't right.

Movement again. The distinct swish of something brushing against nylon. My duffle, sitting on the dresser across from my feet, was being searched. My muscles froze. My brain went to mush, wanting to scream and run, wanting to blend into the blankets, wanting the person to disappear without my having to do anything.

Muffled footsteps walked across carpet. I couldn't sense where they went. My mind rushed to catch up. My purse was on the dresser, near the duffle. Surely the intruder had searched it first. I thought of the gun under the pillow beside me. Thank goodness it hadn't fallen into the prowler's hands — yet. Papers rustled very lightly. About twelve inches from my ear. The intruder was at the night stand beside me. I held my breath.

I caught a sharp intake of breath, his.

"So . . ." the voice whispered raggedly.

I stretched and rolled, hoping to do a reasonable imitation of a sleeping person changing position. My right hand reached for the hidden pistol.

Hands of steel gripped my throat. A knee pinned the blankets down at my side. My eyes bulged, my field of vision narrowing to a small tunnel. Think! I forced myself to remember everything Ron and Drake had taught me about the pistol. The safety was released with a flick of a thumb. It was a double action semi-automatic. I didn't have to cock it, the first shot would require an extra hard squeeze on the trigger, but then it would be ready for more shots.

I struggled to kick free. The dark shape hovered over me, the grip perhaps loosening a tiny bit. Not for long. The attacker renewed his hold, choking off the last of my air. My trapped legs flailing, I managed to get my index finger against the trigger. With only the vaguest sense of direction, I squeezed as hard as I could. The trigger offered massive resistance. My vision blurred. I pulled harder.

The shot deafened me, reverberated endlessly through the room, startled the dark figure into letting go of my throat. I gulped all the air I could grab, my ears ringing with a high steady whine. Finally able to kick free of the restraining blankets, I scrambled to a crouch on the bed, my breath coming in ragged short gasps. My head darted from side to side, as I tried to figure out where he'd gone — where the shot had gone.

The door flew open, slamming into the wall with a crash. The dark figure fled into the rectangle of yellow light outside. I scrambled to my feet, running after him. I threw myself against the door frame, the pistol pointing in the direction he'd gone.

Nothing.

The sidewalk was empty, all the way to the end of the row. Cars sat outside a dozen or so of the rooms. All were silent. A few drapes parted slightly. Lights began popping on in the rooms, although so far none of the inhabitants had ventured out. The phone in my room rang, jarringly and insistently. I backed into the room, keeping the pistol aimed at the open doorway.

"What!" I answered abruptly.

"Miss Parker? Are you all right?" The desk clerk's voice was a curious mixture of sleepy and scared.

"Call the police," I ordered. "My room was broken into."

"Was that a gunshot I heard?" he inquired nervously.

"Get Chief Bradley here. I'll tell him all about it." My voice conveyed a lot more authority than I felt.

I crouched on the bed nearest the back of the room, the one I'd not been sleeping in. Without releasing my grip on the pistol, I propped two pillows against the headboard and sat with my back against them. I faced the open door with gun in hand until I was sure it was Steve Bradley's silhouette I saw there.

Flicking the safety on, I set the gun carefully on the bed, the barrel pointing away from either Bradley or myself. I reached over and switched on the bedside lamp. My eyes squinted at the sudden intrusion but they quickly adjusted.

"I'll have to take this," Bradley said, reaching for the pistol.

"You'll find it's been fired once — by me," I told him.

I quickly outlined the sequence of events.

"I haven't touched anything since he left," I said.

"You sure it was a 'he'?"

Was I? I thought about the figure. Average height, slim build. Dressed in dark clothing, probably jeans and a dark sweater or sweatshirt.

"I can't imagine a woman having that kind of strength in her hands," I told him.

"Your neck's not broken," he reminded me. "A very strong man could have probably done that."

I reached up to touch my throat carefully. My fingers stopped just short. "Can you get fingerprints off skin?" I asked.

"It can be done," he said, "but I have a feeling this one was wearing gloves."

I tried to think again of the attack. Gloved hands or bare? I couldn't say for sure. All I'd been thinking about at the time was how to fire the gun.

Bradley was following my thoughts. He clicked on a small flashlight, shining it over the walls and ceiling.

"Any idea where the bullet went?" he asked.

I crawled over to the mussed bed, showing him where I'd been and trying to approximate my position.

"The attacker was there," I told him, indicating the edge of the bed near the nightstand. "I rolled to my back like so," I said, rolling. "By that time, I thought I was going to die and I really wasn't thinking about where the shot would go."

"Well, at least you've had good training," he commented, still scanning the walls. "You fired a warning shot."

I did? Wisely, I didn't mention to Bradley that I would have killed the sonofabitch dead if I could have. He was just damn lucky I'd had no chance to aim.

"Hmm, look at this," Bradley said. He was picking at a dark spot on the wall which divided the small closet alcove from the main section of the room.

I stayed on the bed with no desire to nose into the new find. I felt suddenly drained of energy.

He continued to pick at the drywall, digging into the small hole with narrow pliers he had unfolded from some tool on his belt.

"Look at this," he said again.

I was finding it tiresome. I would have rather seen him run out the door and down the sidewalk after the intruder.

"Looks like the bullet went into the wall and got stopped by the metal bracket on this hanging rack on the other side."

"How interesting," I said snidely. "I know I fired a bullet, I know it went that way, I'm glad to hear it didn't go through any critical walls into anyone else's room. Now can we ask some real questions? Like how did he get into the room. I *had* fastened the door chain. Who is it and where did he go?"

I left out the important one. *Why?* Why would someone come after me?

"Listen, missy, you're damn lucky you didn't kill someone here," he waved an index finger in my direction. "You could be facing a lot more than a sleepless night right now."

His adamance crumbled me. My face puckered and my eyes stung. I blinked twice and swallowed hard.

"Look, I'm sorry," he relented. "We've got a fingerprint man on the way over. We'll check the room, although in a motel . . . well, you know there's been dozens of people in and out. Finding something won't guarantee we get our man, or, uh, person."

I breathed deeply, aware for the first time that my throat ached. "I know."

A tentative knock sounded at the doorjamb. The desk clerk's stringy brown hair showed first, even before his thin face peeked around the edge of the open door. He glanced at me on the bed, then at Bradley, who was still holding the chalky bullet.

"You need me for anything?" he asked nervously.

"Another officer will come around for your statement," Bradley told him. "It might be tomorrow. I can't drag too many officers out of bed this late."

For the first time, I glanced at the clock. Two a.m. No wonder I felt so wrung out. I'd only had about two hours sleep.

"For now, you can arrange another room for Miss Parker to finish the night in," Bradley was telling the clerk.

The man nodded. His eyes went for the first time to the doorjamb. His fingers lifted the dangling end of the broken chain.

"Looks like they cut this," he commented.

Bradley spoke up. "Yeah, I figured they had a key or a master, got the door open quietly, then snipped the chain with bolt cutters.

Couldn'ta done that with deadbolts on the doors, you know," he added, giving the clerk a direct stare.

"Hey, man, it ain't my place," he defended. "I only work here." He backed away.

"We'll get some more answers on that later," Bradley said to me. "Look, you oughta get some sleep. Why don't you gather up your stuff."

Like I was really going to fall asleep. So many questions.

I went into the bathroom and tossed my few toilet articles into my zippered makeup bag. Suddenly I realized that I'd been walking around in nothing but panties and a large T-shirt. Edging my way back into the room, I picked up the jeans and bra I'd discarded earlier in the evening and slipped back into the bathroom to dress.

It took only a couple of minutes to throw all my other possessions into the duffle. I turned to Bradley.

"My gun please," I said, holding out my hand.

He had set it on the dresser. He glanced down at it, then back at me. A flicker of uncertainty darted across his mouth.

"I really should keep it as evidence," he began.

"And let this guy come back for me? Steve, be real here. I'm supposed to check into another room in the same motel, another room with the same lousy little chain at the door, and just let him come back? You know the minute your police cars leave here, I'm fair game again. You know I'm in no shape to drive back home." I felt my voice rise with each point, my vocal chords tightening painfully.

"Okay, okay," he pacified. "You go to your new room. You lock yourself in. Put something against the door. Don't open it before daylight for any reason."

His finger jabbed the dresser top as he talked. "You got that?"

I nodded without too much feeling.

"I want you to come to the station in the morning and let the clerk take your statement. Then I think you'd be wise to leave this town."

"Is that an order?"

"You acted in self defense. I have no evidence, yet, that this was nothing more than a random burglary attempt. I can't make you leave. But, lady, you're crazy if you don't." He wagged his head slowly.

I gritted my teeth, working at a response, when a tap sounded at the door.

"We can put you in 102," the clerk interrupted. "It's right next to the office. I'll be right on the other side of the wall."

Not a terribly comforting thought, but it would have to do.

"Leave your car parked outside this room," Steve Bradley suggested. "We don't need to advertise where you're spending the rest of the night."

That made sense anyway. I picked up the pistol and the packed duffle, then scanned the room to be sure I hadn't forgotten anything. Bradley nodded a goodbye as I followed the clerk out the door. My eyes darted around the parking area, quiet now, and the darkened windows of the other rooms. The other guests had apparently decided that sleep was more important than the brief intrusion that had interrupted it. We cut across the parking lot to the opposite leg of the L shaped building and the clerk unlocked the door to the room adjoining the motel office.

"Any chance I could get a cup of tea?" I asked as he handed me the key. All I could think of now was comfort food.

"Well," he hedged, "the coffee and rolls won't be set out until seven."

"Look, I was nearly strangled a little while ago. Couldn't you just microwave a cup of water and toss a tea bag into it?"

He seemed to sense that it really wasn't an unreasonable request, given that he'd gotten off incredibly easy already. After all, he didn't have any dead bodies to deal with and the press hadn't shown up. Yet.

"I'll bring your tea in a minute," he offered with an almost sympathetic hint in his voice.

I switched on the light in the room, dumped my duffle on the dresser, and kept the pistol in hand until I'd thoroughly checked the premises. It was identical to the room I'd just vacated, right down to the dark blue commercial grade carpeting.

"Here you are, ma'am." He'd placed a styrofoam cup of steaming water on a small tray. Beside it lay a paper-wrapped tea bag. "There's extra hot water in this big cup," he said, indicating a larger lidded cup.

"Thanks, that's very nice of you," I told him.

"Now you lock yourself in," he said, "and don't worry. I'll be right next door." He did seem concerned.

I set the tea tray on the dresser and locked and chained the door. As an additional precaution, I pulled one of the straight-backed chairs from the small round table by the window and wedged it beneath the doorknob. I found myself looking around for things to do. Debated about unpacking, decided that was useless. I'd only be here, let's see, another three or four hours.

I dunked the tea bag in the steaming water, absentmindedly dipping it a dozen times or so until I had concocted a black brew that rivaled coffee. Decided that would definitely keep me awake for a day or two, so I proceeded to perform a little pouring back and forth ritual between the stiff black brew and the spare cup of hot water, like a scientist with an important experiment. In reality, I was working hard at avoiding the thoughts that lurked at the periphery of my brain.

Who just tried to choke the shit out of me? I rubbed gently at my neck as I carried the now-drinkable tea to the nightstand and settled myself into the puffed pillows against the headboard. My mind rambled over the day. Who had I managed to frighten?

Because I had to believe that was at the bottom of this. Someone was running scared.

22

The hot tea soothed my aching throat and eased my nerves into a semblance of calm. I thought back over the places I'd been today. Lunch with Laura Armijo. We'd talked about Richard Martinez and Laura had given me a list of women who'd miscarried. I'd stopped off at Mary McDonald's. I could hardly remember the specifics of the conversation. The clinic? The battered women's group? I thought of the little place where I'd eaten dinner. The proprietress, Sal, had been pretty chatty. And there was that lone man sitting at the other end of the room. Maybe he'd overheard. Maybe he worked for someone whose nerves I'd touched. Maybe I was becoming extremely paranoid.

I took a deep breath and got up to use the bathroom. It was after four a.m. and I didn't feel the least bit sleepy. My mind was still racing over the possibilities, and checking off my routine of the day didn't seem to make it slow down. I soaked a washcloth in hot water and held it to my face, willing the tension to leave my skin and soak into the fabric. The puzzle was coming no closer to resolution.

I hung the washcloth on a chrome bar and slipped out of my jeans. Crawling between the sheets, I switched on the television, leaving the volume low. I finished the last of the tea, switched off the lamp, and begged for sleep to overtake me. My eyes stayed wide open. An old movie ended and another started. I tried to follow the story, in hopes that my thoughts could be put on hold for awhile. I woke up sometime around six, with maybe an hour's worth of sleep to my credit.

My head felt light and empty. I couldn't remember exactly what had kept me awake all night. The attack had lost its terror, feeling unreal in daylight. None of the tangle of thoughts that occupied me in the darkness ever coalesced into a firm decision. I pulled myself from under the covers and headed for the shower.

My Jeep waited across the nearly empty parking lot. I carried all my possessions out in one trip, leaving the room key on the dresser. A substantial breakfast sounded good before I had to face giving a statement at the police station. I drove back to Sal's, where I'd eaten dinner last night.

Sal herself was on duty, again the lone waitress.

"Hey, you're back," she greeted. "Good to see you again."

She splashed coffee into a cup without spilling a drop. I ordered a veggie omelette, wheat toast, and a fruit cup, feeling quite righteous for avoiding the sausage, bacon, and fried pota- toes.

It was still early and the place was, once again, not crowded. I wondered if Sal was really making a living out of it. A couple occupied a booth down the row from mine, but they seemed completely involved with only each other. Like Drake and I might have been, had he been here with me.

"Sal? You got a minute?" I asked when she passed by.

She glanced at the other couple, making sure they were all right. "Sure," she said. She slid into the booth across from me and set the coffee pot between us.

"Remember what we were talking about last night?" I asked.

She squinted her eyes together, thinking. "About Cynthia Martinez?"

"Yeah. Well, I was wondering . . . " Wondering how to phrase a question or two without telling her about my evening. Information which might easily be all over town by noon if I told her. "Did you tell anyone else about that conversation?"

She pulled her chest up straighter. "I don't make a habit of gossip," she answered formally.

"Oh, I didn't mean that," I assured her, although I wasn't the least bit sure of her assertion. "I just, well, it's kind of touchy."

She sat very still.

"I mean, I think someone's after me."

She leaned in closer. "What do you mean, honey?"

I really didn't want to elaborate. "Oh, I don't know, Sal. I just, well . . . " I was not handling this well at all. "Remember that man who sat at the other end of the room? Do you know him well?"

"Larry? Sure. He's lived in town all his life. Runs a little appliance repair shop down next to that car dealer that sells them little small cars."

"He's not dangerous, is he?"

She burst out laughing, attracting glances from the couple in the other booth. They smiled and went back to their conversation. "Oh, heavens no," she breathed. "Larry's one of the sweetest men you'd ever know."

"Okay, well, never mind then," I said, hoping to cut off any other questions. I felt a bit foolish but didn't really know where else to turn.

Sal got up to check the other's coffee and I finished my breakfast quickly. I left cash on the table and walked out into another sunny day.

The police station was just coming awake as I drove up. Steve Bradley had apparently opted to come in late after his middle-of-the-night call from me. I was escorted into a private room where I gave a statement to an officer who didn't seem to have a very clear idea of why I was there. He didn't ask many questions, simply took down what I told him and had me sign the form when finished.

Thirty minutes later I found myself outside again, with no definitive plan for the day. Bradley's warning from last night came back to me. He wanted me out of town. Unfortunately, more than ever, I wanted answers.

The fact that someone had gone to the trouble to break into my room, search my things, then try to kill me, told me that I was getting close to something. I only wished I knew what.

The day was getting warm already, even though it was not yet nine o'clock. I climbed back into the Jeep and rolled all the windows down. The sun had topped the surrounding mountains early and now scoured the sky a pale blue. Dust settled on the trees and shrubs. The grayish chamisa which grew around the perimeter of the police station parking lot looked as if it survived on a steady diet of the powdery brown stuff. A small patch of yellow and orange marigolds near the doorway provided the brightest spot of color on the property. I noticed them but my mind was mulling over my options.

I started the car and cruised aimlessly up the main street of the sleepy little town. Saturday morning. People were only beginning to stir. Traffic was light, almost non-existent by Albuquerque standards. Most of the visible cars were clustered around restaurants and gas stations. The variety store had apparently just opened because parking spaces near the front door were still plentiful. The clinic was quiet. Only two cars sat in the lot, much the same arrangement as the first time Sally and I had come here, although I couldn't be sure if they were the same vehicles. I noticed that their Saturday hours were posted as nine to three.

Nothing here was giving me the answers I needed and with a sudden burst of longing for my own home and my own dog, I hung a U at the next intersection and headed south. Ninety-four minutes later I pulled into my driveway. Rusty bounded out of Elsa's back door and nearly skidded around the blue spruce at the corner of the house in his haste to greet me. I hugged him with something nearing desperation. Suddenly, every bit of adrenalin drained from my body and I could think of nothing but a nice long sleep.

Dropping my purse and duffle on the living room floor behind the couch, I stripped on the way down the hall and turned the shower on hot. Within ten minutes, I had closed the drapes, taken the phone off the hook, and slipped into bed. When I stretched lazily and turned toward the nightstand, the clock said it was five p.m. I rolled away from it and stretched again. The sheets were cool and smooth and reminded me that Drake had been gone three days now.

Six-thirty. The red numerals stared at me and I stared back at them. I must have dozed again, but somehow it felt like I'd been thinking the whole time. I allowed myself the luxury of lying there briefly, until a new thought struck me. Had my nighttime intruder stolen anything?

I vaguely remembered Steve Bradley asking that question and I thought I'd responded negatively. The hands appeared empty when the dark shape dashed through the door. But I hadn't checked. I'd no idea how long the person had been in my room before I awoke. No idea how thoroughly they'd searched my purse and duffle. With sudden purpose, I got out of bed. Pulled on a pair of panties and a robe, then retrieved the duffle and purse from behind the couch in the living room. I pawed through them, looking for my notes, anything that might prove incriminating.

Everything appeared to be intact. Even the small spiral with my notes, the names Laura had given me at lunch. I smoothed the bedspread and dumped the contents of both bags. My purse was the usual disaster — wallet, keys, lipstick, and business cards, all held together with a collection of paper scraps, loose coins, unwrapped dinner mints, and nameless fuzz. I picked through the good items, dusting them off. The wallet still contained money, credit cards and ID. I couldn't tell that anything was missing.

One by one, I replaced the purse contents while tossing aside the scrap junk. After discarding the used shopping lists, cellophane candy wrappers, and unidentified lint, I came up with just one unfamiliar item. A tiny cup-shaped thing, slightly larger than a contact lens. I carried it to the window and opened the drape.

It was opaque white, flexible. As I examined it more closely, I noticed a ragged tear at one edge. It had caught on something inside the purse, probably the keychain, then torn cleanly away. Away from the fingertip of a latex glove. Like a surgical glove. My skin prickled.

23

My mind whirled. I tried to remember the figure of the intruder as he'd escaped my room. Someone from the clinic. Definitely not Chris, the receptionist, although she was the one I'd talked to the most. She was far shorter and plumper than the silhouette I'd seen. And I seriously doubted that she possessed the iron strength of those hands that had wrapped around my neck.

The doctors? I shook my head to clear it. The idea seemed so implausible. My heart thumped as an idea began to form.

Something about the questions I'd been asking had frightened someone. The answer had to be in the patient files. I had to get back into that clinic. My hands shook slightly as I selected black leggings and an oversized navy blue cotton sweater from a dresser drawer. My mind raced. Black socks and shoes, a pair of gloves. I rounded them up. What on earth was I thinking?

It would be dark in an hour. I could be in and out of the clinic by ten and home again by midnight. Was I totally crazy?

Rummaging through my kitchen junk drawer, I gathered a few basic tools, including a can of black shoe polish that I envisioned smearing camouflage-style on my face. I tossed all the tools and extra clothing into the duffle. Rusty stared at me quizzically, ears cocked and head tilted.

"Don't worry," I assured him, "you get to come, too."

I should let someone know where I was going. Who? Gram would be no help. She could dial 911, but if my plan failed, how would she get them to Valle Escondido in time to do me any good? Ron? I wasn't eager for a lecture.

I paced through the house, trying to think. I should make it look like I was home. I pulled drapes and turned on lamps. I should leave a message on the answering machine at the office. I called, knowing that if I wasn't home by morning, it might not matter anyway. I should have my head examined.

Rusty scampered alongside me out to the Jeep, completely unaware of the crazy stunt I was about to get us into. We stopped for gas at the edge of town. Traffic was heavy, like everyone in town was eager to get out and everyone from out of town was headed in. The sun turned the western sky to fire as I passed the exits leading to each of the Indian pueblos. Spangled signs at each turnoff enticed the traveler toward the glittering casinos.

By the time I hit the outskirts of Santa Fe the sun had disappeared, relieving the glare considerably. Realizing that I hadn't eaten anything since the veggie omelette this morning, I pulled off at Cerrillos Road, found a fast-food drive through, and cruised on out. On the Interstate again, Rusty and I ate our cheeseburgers and fries.

The lights of Valle Escondido sparkled below as we topped a small rise about a mile out of town. I glanced around nervously as we entered the town. Strange cars were easily spotted here, although mine was hardly a stranger any more. I felt like eyes were watching me. I cruised past the clinic once, staring openly, checking it carefully. No cars in the lot, muted lighting in the lobby. The rest of the building was dark.

I turned left at the next side street, then left again almost immediately into an alley. Prayed that it backed the clinic. I passed the back of a small strip center. All the metal doors were unmarked, with trash cans beside them. A beat up compact car sat outside one of the doors. A business owner working late Saturday night or the cleaning people? Either way, I'd have to be careful not to attract attention. The other side of the alley backed on residences, separated by a solid looking block wall.

Halogen lights around the parking lot illuminated the back of the clinic. Small spotlights on the ground lit the shrubbery. These people sure were paranoid about nighttime intruders. I drove past and found a dark spot about two doors down, well out of sight of the parked compact car.

Rusty rushed the door eagerly when I stopped, but I managed to restrain him.

"Not just yet, boy," I cautioned. "I think I have to go this one alone."

I rummaged into the duffle bag. Tucked a flashlight, screwdriver, and the dark gloves into the pockets of my sweater. The can of black shoe polish looked up at me. I decided I had no idea what was in that stuff and worried that it might never come off my skin — decided against painting myself with it.

Rusty watched curiously. I tried to think what the hell I was going to do next.

I took a deep breath. "Okay, kid, you're gonna guard the car for me. If I'm not back in half an hour, you call for help."

He wagged to thank me for my faith in him. I left the windows down about two inches each and locked the doors. The red-brown face with cocked ears turned toward me inquisitively. I hoped he wouldn't bark when I got out of sight.

Glancing around, I pasted myself into the shadow of the building. No movement. Soft light glowed from the residential windows behind the block wall. No curtains moved. I waited two minutes then edged my way to the side of my protective wall.

The clinic stood alone, surrounded by a much too open parking lot, its tan walls glowing nearly gold. The back door looked metal and solid. The aluminum framed windows were dark and covered by curlicued wrought iron bars. How on earth was I going to get into the place? I rubbed my temples.

The lighting was far too bright. I edged around the building where I stood until I could see down the side of the clinic to the street. Traffic was light but steady. No way I'd get around to the front without being seen. I eyed the light pole beside me.

It took three throws but I finally managed a strategically placed rock. The crash sent me ducking into the bushes. Two minutes later, I sneaked a peek out. No voices shouted, no doors were flung open, no sirens blared. And the back corner of the parking lot was now pleasantly, comfortingly dark.

I glanced to the rear corner of the clinic. A small spotlight on the ground illuminated the surrounding shrubbery. Confidently, I licked my lips. Piece of cake.

Out of sight of the street once again, I scanned the entire area quickly. Clear. I dashed for the side of the clinic, ducking behind a three foot arbor vitae. Directly in front of me, a yellow-pink footlight glared straight into my face. That seemed reason enough to administer a swift kick to it. The resulting darkness wasn't total, but was certainly better than before. I felt reasonably confident that I could work without being easily seen.

I turned to examine the metal back door. Slipped my dark gloves on before touching anything. The knob was cool and smooth and very firmly locked. A deadbolt lock above it reinforced the door's impenetrability. No one had been considerate enough to leave it unlocked for me. I directed my attention to the windows on either side of the door.

The wrought iron bars looked strong. I grabbed one of them and shook it. Not the slightest movement. I crossed to the other window and repeated the exercise. This one rattled just a little; there was perhaps a quarter inch play where the bars on the left side attached to the stuccoed wall. The fire escape. I wasn't up on the local fire codes in every town, but this just might be my chance. Some places required that at least one rear and one front window be unobstructed. If so, this might be the one. The bars would extend through the wall and be fastened by large wing nuts on the inside. Anyone trapped inside could quickly undo the wing nuts. The wrought iron grating would be hinged on one side and could swing open like a small door. A quick examination of the right hand side of the grate confirmed the presence of hinges. Okay.

The window itself consisted of two large glass panes, aluminum framed with a very basic latch holding them in the center. I pressed my hands against the glass, watching it bow inward. This shouldn't be too difficult. If I could wedge my screwdriver in and move the latch, I should be able to slide the glass open, then reach in and unfasten the wing nuts, giving myself an entrance.

It worked. Until the glass slid open and the burglar alarm went off.

24

Oh, shit. I froze.

The incessant jangling filled the night air, echoing off the other buildings. I tucked myself back behind the safety of the arbor vitae. My heart pounded and sweat froze on my body.

A couple of drapes in the residences pulled open to reveal curious faces looking out. Seeing nothing, the faces retreated and the drapes fell back into place. I thought longingly of my Jeep and my dog, parked a hundred yards away out of sight.

Two full minutes that felt like two full hours passed. I looked around again. The houses were all still, the traffic had not all come to a stop. Neighborhood was pretty well ignoring the blaring alarm. I had to get out of there.

My knee joints crackled as I rose. I took a deep breath and ran for the shadow of the nearest building, edged my way around it, and straightened my shoulders to walk nonchalantly to my Jeep. Where Steve Bradley waited, leaning against his patrol car.

His arms were folded across his chest and not the faintest trace of a smile showed anywhere on his face.

"You don't listen real well, do you?" he drawled.

I couldn't think of a response to that.

"I told you to leave this alone, didn't I? I told you to go home." His arms had dropped to his sides and he'd taken two steps toward me. "What the hell are you doing here?"

The screaming alarm seemed to answer that question.

"Didn't your mama ever tell you that two wrongs don't make a right? You think you're getting back at someone for the break-in at your motel room last night?" His index finger was aimed at my nose.

I opened my mouth to respond, but two more squad cars roared up with lights and sirens filling the night. All the residential windows were lit now, with dark silhouettes peering out. A couple of the back doors opened and a few curious souls stood on their porches to witness the big fuss.

Two officers, a male and a female, jumped out of the cars, leaving the blue and red lights bouncing off the buildings and pavement. The quiet neighborhood was beginning to feel like the inside of a disco.

The male officer had his hand on the butt of his gun as he approached. Bradley gave a tiny negative shake of his head.

"Go check out the clinic, Jim," he ordered. Jim gave me another suspicious look before heading to do as the chief ordered.

"How did you get here so quickly?" I ventured to ask.

"The alarm rings at the station. I was sitting down at the next intersection when I got the radio call."

Nowhere in the world were the police this efficient. Just my luck. The blaring alarm stopped just then, leaving a silent void. Officer Jim must have the keys.

"I can't just let you go with a warning," Bradley sighed. "Do you know how much paperwork you've just created?"

The female officer, M. Martinez according to her name badge, had circled me in the meantime. She placed my hands on the hood of her car and proceeded to pat down my sides and legs. The screwdriver came out of my sweater pocket and was handed over to Bradley. The neighbors were practically taking notes by now. For the first time in my life, I had an idea why people being hauled off by the police always covered their faces. I felt like a sideshow attraction.

Officer Jim came back and briefly explained to Bradley about the open window and broken spotlight. M. Martinez started to snap handcuffs onto my wrists.

"Not necessary," Steve Bradley told her, "just take her to the station."

"What about my car and my dog?" I felt panic rising. I was supposed to be home safe by midnight.

He glanced uncertainly toward Rusty. The dog smiled back, his little characteristic grin that comes off looking like a snarl. Bradley stepped back.

"I'll call animal control."

"No!" A flame of terror shot up my throat. "No, please. He's harmless. Let him come to the station with me."

The three officers glanced at each other, some silent communication passing between them.

"You got a leash for the dog?" Bradley asked.

I had to think. "Yes, in the back seat."

"Get it."

Officer Martinez held out my car keys to me. I unlocked the door, holding Rusty back. I clipped the leash to his collar and let him out. The three police officers made nice-nice noises to him and he promptly licked each of their hands. Convinced that I didn't have a killer beast with me, they ushered the two of us into the back seat of the cruiser.

"I'll drive your car in," Steve said, taking the keys from me. "You really are a pain in the ass," he grumbled.

Martinez mercifully turned off the flashing lights and we headed quietly toward the police station. Rusty stared out the side window. The neighbors stood in little clusters, comparing notes. I felt like I might throw up.

Glaring fluorescent lights in the station lent an unreal air to the next hours. I felt lightheaded as they ushered me and Rusty inside, filled out forms, took fingerprints, and informed me that I had rights and should call an attorney. Right now, I couldn't think who I would call — certainly not Ron just yet. I wanted to talk to Bradley, to explain my reasons for being here. My logical side told me that probably wasn't smart, but my logical side wasn't in control right now.

A big round utilitarian clock on the wall showed that it was after midnight. Rusty lay on the brown and white tile floor, his head on his paws. I was slumped into a wooden chair, my eyes feeling extremely heavy, my mind numb. Officer Martinez seemed to be the only other person here right now. She bustled about, putting my forms into a manila folder, opening drawers, locking them.

"You ought to get some sleep," she said. "Come on."

I followed her and Rusty followed me through a doorway and down a hall. Four small cells flanked the hall. They were all empty. The keys rattled as she unlocked the first door and ushered us in. A metal bed frame stood in one corner with a blue and white striped mattress rolled up on the wire springs. The bed, a tiny sink, and a stainless steel toilet in the opposite corner were the only furnishings. The metal bars clanged hollowly as she closed the door behind us. Tears welled in my eyes as her footsteps echoed away.

I unrolled the mattress and sat down. Rusty sat beside me, his head in my lap. Prisoners.

Somewhere in the distance, I could hear a typewriter clipping along. Otherwise, the place was dead quiet. I looked at the white sheet that covered the mattress. It appeared clean, had presumably been washed after the last resident left, but I couldn't bring myself to put my head on it. I leaned my back against the wall and Rusty jumped up beside me. He curled into a large red-brown circle and I sank down to rest my head on him.

There's something very comforting about being snuggled up close with a warm, although doggy-smelling, friend. I must have dozed because the next time I looked at my watch three hours had gone by. Pretending I'd had a full night's sleep, my mind went into full-alert. Much as I wanted to drift off to sleep again and forget everything that had happened, I couldn't get my eyes to close again.

I stretched, disturbing the dog. He stretched, too, and we both stood up. With no qualms about manners, he walked over and took a long drink from the toilet. I felt sort of dry myself, but wasn't willing to go that far. I ran the water in the little sink until it was nearly cold, then splashed my face. I sipped from my cupped hand and pretended that it was what I really wanted.

M. Martinez had kept pretty well to herself. Occasionally, I heard the phone ring and her muffled voice answered it. Where was Bradley? I desperately needed to talk to him — something I should have done before going to the clinic. If I'd shown him the torn surgical glove, chances were good that I might have convinced him to search the place himself, or at least to question the doctors about the break-in at my motel room. As it was, I looked like the criminal. I shuddered to think just how viciously the doctors would press charges against me.

My mind raced over various subjects. Where was my purse now? The little glove fragment was in there. I tried to put the previous night into order. I'd had the purse in the squad car, but thought they took it and put it into a personal effects bag here at the station.

What actual evidence had they found at the scene? I'd worn gloves when I touched the window. I wasn't sure how they would prove that I'd been the person who broke the lights. Should I deny everything? If I had an attorney, I felt sure that he'd advise me to stay quiet. Or plead insanity, clearly the best choice in light of what I'd done.

The cell was quiet in a hollow way. From the front office, the sounds of salsa music drifted softly back. Officer M. must have switched on the radio for company. I kept checking my watch, wondering what time Bradley would be in. Was he still investigating the crime scene, or was he finished for the night, not due to return until the morning shift? What about Officer Jim? I didn't really want to answer to him. I paced.

Rusty paced with me a few times, then gave up and flopped on the floor. After awhile, he decided that was too hard and cold and he jumped back onto the bed. I finally decided that I wasn't accomplishing anything either, so I joined him.

This time, I made him move to one end and I stretched out on my back. The lighting consisted of two recessed bulbs in the hallway, leaving the cell itself in dimness. It was easy to drift back to sleep again. The next thing I knew, M. was bringing in a styrofoam carton that smelled wonderfully of bacon and eggs.

Rusty's leash was stuffed into one of her pants pockets. In one move, she handed me the styrofoam breakfast tray while reaching for the leash and clipping it to Rusty's collar with the other.

"Time for you to take a little run outside," she said to the dog.

I decided it would probably be the most private time for me to avail myself of the meager facilities here, too. I managed it in the very short time Rusty and M. were outside.

"What about Rusty's food?" I asked.

"I don't suppose you brought anything for him," she asked.

"Well, I hadn't really planned on being here for breakfast," I told her.

She glanced around uncertainly. "I'll radio the chief and have him bring some dog food when he comes in."

"And maybe a bowl for water," I suggested. "He, uh, wants to drink from the toilet."

She flashed me a thoroughly disgusted look as she left.

"Hey, I didn't teach him that habit," I grumbled as her back passed through the door to the office.

I sat on the edge of the bed and opened the styrofoam container. Scrambled eggs, three strips of bacon, four triangles of toast, and a one-inch square plastic tub of jelly. A plastic fork but no knife. They obviously couldn't take the chance that I'd use it to pull a jailbreak.

Rusty sat at my feet, head tilted and ears perked toward the food. He licked his lips about every three seconds. I slipped him one of the toast triangles and broke one of the bacon strips into small pieces. These I tossed across the cell to him between taking bites of egg. He wolfed them down.

"Hey, slow down," I told him. "You'll get a full meal later, you know."

I wondered where I'd eat *my* next meal. The idea of spending more time here wasn't that appealing.

M. appeared about thirty minutes later to collect the dishes and count the silverware.

"Hey . . . well, what's your name, anyway? I can't just call you M."

"Officer Martinez will work," she answered. "First name's Melissa."

"Thanks, Melissa. Any relationship to Cynthia and Richard Martinez?"

"Everybody here's related," she smiled. "Richard is my father's second cousin."

"Oh. Hey, what's the procedure for getting out of here?" I asked. "How much longer do I get to be a ward of the state?"

"Usually there's a hearing before the judge, he sets or denies bail, and we take it from there."

"Judge?" This was getting more complicated by the minute. Maybe I *should* call Ron and arrange a lawyer. "When will that be?"

"Well, today's Sunday. He comes to town on Tuesdays and Thursdays."

"Tuesday?" My voice squeaked slightly as I edged the word out. My stomach had a heavy feeling that couldn't be entirely attributed to the eggs.

She shrugged.

"When will the chief be in?" I asked.

She checked the watch on her wrist. "In about an hour," she said.

"I really, really need to talk to him," I said. "Can you send him back here as soon as he gets in?"

"Sure. Everything else okay?"

Well, I could use my toothbrush, a change of clothes, a hot shower, and some shampoo. A massage would be nice. "Fine," I grumbled. "Everything's fine." I sank down on the cot again.

Rusty clicked his way across the cell to stick his head out through the bars and watch Melissa Martinez leave. He liked having the ability to look up and down the small corridor, so he stayed that way. I'd always envisioned being incarcerated as the perfect chance to kick back with a stack of good books and a two-pound box of Russell Stover, with no pressures, no telephones, no one pulling for my attention.

It wasn't turning out that way.

Ron probably wouldn't go in to the office until Monday, so he wouldn't know about the message I'd left on the machine. The judge wouldn't be here until Tuesday to decide that I wasn't such a hardened criminal that I might be trusted out on the streets again. Or that I should spend my life behind bars. I still had a phone call coming. I could call Ron, but I didn't look forward to it.

How would I ever explain this?

Steve Bradley arrived to find me in the same position, sitting on the cot, tapping my fingers against my knee. Rusty pulled his head back inside the cell and began waving his tail back and forth slowly. Bradley greeted him with a gentle tone, sending the tail into vigorous sweeps. The chief reached through the bars to scratch the dog's ears.

"Officer Martinez said you wanted to talk to me," he began.

"I have proof that the doctors at the clinic are somehow connected to the break-in at my motel room."

"Now why on earth would you think that?" he asked. "Why would a doctor need to go breaking into the motel rooms of strangers?"

I explained about finding the small piece of surgical glove in my purse. "If you'll go get the purse, I'll show it to you," I told him.

His brows pulled together in front. "Was anything missing from your bags?" he asked.

"No, and that's the puzzling thing. I had some notes in there with names to check out. It's still there. I'm not sure why the intruder went through my things. Maybe he really meant to kill me. He sure tried hard enough, and if I hadn't had that pistol with me I'd be dead by now."

"But one of the doctors? I just don't get it."

I didn't either, but my goal right now was to get out of jail before Tuesday.

"What were you doing at the clinic?" he asked.

The moment of truth. Talk or insist on a lawyer? I couldn't see much point in trying to weasel out of something I'd done.

"What are the charges, chief?" I asked.

"Destruction of property. Attempted burglary."

"If I pay for the damages, can I get out of here? I didn't actually steal anything and had no intention of stealing anything. I wanted to sneak a look at a couple of patient files to see if my suspicions are correct."

"What suspicions?" he asked.

I hesitated. "I really can't say. What if they turn out to be unfounded?"

His steady eyes met mine and didn't let go.

"Okay, I wanted to know if the doctors were hiding evidence of spouse abuse. If they were protecting some of the men in this town."

"Now why would they do that, ma'am?" His West Texas was showing again.

"I don't know! Maybe they're buddies at the country club." I knew it was a reasonable question, but I wasn't feeling very reasonable right now. "Can you question them? Find out if that's the case?"

"Based on what evidence? That someone broke into your room, tried to strangle you, and that you later found a small piece of latex in your purse? Even if they admitted covering for these men, what would I do about it? There's doctor-patient confidentiality. And unless the women wanted to press charges, I couldn't arrest anyone."

"What about my nearly broken neck? You could arrest someone for that."

"They aren't very likely to admit it, and I sure as hell don't have any proof."

"So, how can I get out of here?" I brought the conversation back to the original subject.

"Wait until Tuesday for the judge."

I rubbed my temples, pressing hard, trailing my fingers across my eyes.

"Or, I could release you because we don't have enough evidence to hold you."

My head snapped up. "You could? Really?" I jumped up and covered the three feet to the bars in one step. Gripping the bars like a hardened criminal, I did my best to appeal to him.

"I don't want you to leave town just yet," he said. "And I'll want to check out that piece of latex you found."

"Gladly. Anything." I knew I sounded desperate.

He pulled a keyring from his pocket and unlocked the cell. Rusty and I lunged for the hall at the same time.

"Easy now," Bradley assured me. "Come on up front and let's get this all straight."

At his desk, he pulled out a small sack of dry dog food. "I didn't know what kind he liked," he said, pouring a generous helping into a clean plastic butter tub and setting it down for Rusty.

The dog gobbled at the food, reassuring Bradley that his choice had been a good one. While Rusty ate, the chief opened a desk drawer and pulled out the large packet containing my personal effects. My purse, car keys, dark gloves, and screwdriver fell out. I eagerly reached for the purse and found the tiny piece of latex.

He took it and slipped it into a plastic evidence bag. For all the good it would do. I pulled out my wallet and handed him a few dollars.

"For the dog food," I said. "I'll pay for the broken lights, too."

"Let's wait on that," he told me. "As long as I have your word that you won't leave town for a couple of days. Officially, the judge should hear this and set a fine."

"Okay. Deal."

"Where will you stay?" he asked.

I thought of the Ponderosa Inn and wasn't too crazy about going there. "Can I use your phone?"

He passed it to me.

"And telephone book?"

I looked up Mary McDonald's number and dialed. She seemed happy to hear from me, surprised that it had been less than two days since the last time we talked. She had an available room for two nights and I told her I'd take it. I told Bradley where

I'd be, then took my belongings, my well-fed dog, and myself out the back door to the spot where he indicated they'd parked my Jeep. Sitting once again in my own set of wheels, with the freedom to drive away, felt incredibly good.

25

The black leggings and dark sweater that I'd chosen last night were oppressive in the July heat. Not to mention that they were dirty and sticky feeling, and I didn't at all want to spend the next two days in the same clothes I'd slept in in a jail cell. I debated what to do about it.

It was still only a little after nine a.m., the sun high already, the air still. Traffic was non-existent as I pulled onto the main drag. The town variety store looked deserted but I pulled into the parking lot to check out their hours, hoping like crazy that they would be open on Sunday. Nine-thirty, the sign told me — not too long to wait. I took the parking spot directly in front of the door, just so someone inside would realize that they already had a customer. I had begun to doze slightly when a few other cars arrived and joined the wait. It wasn't long.

I purchased a toothbrush, toothpaste, hair brush, two pair of panties, some cheap sandals, and a couple of cotton short and T-shirt sets they had on sale. My cash was running low and I hoped Bradley wouldn't drag this visit out too long. If I had to appear before the judge on Tuesday, I'd have to think of something appropriate to wear. I really hoped we'd have the entire episode behind us by then.

Mary's driveway held two strange cars with out of state plates when I arrived. I realized belatedly that it was still early and she might not be finished serving breakfast yet. I hesitated in the drive before finding a parking spot.

Mary must have spotted me from the window, because she came out onto the porch and waved me in. I made Rusty wait in the car until I could assess the situation.

"Come on in," Mary invited, giving me a warm hug.

"I didn't even stop to think that your guests would still be here," I apologized.

"No problem," she assured me. "One group is just getting ready to go. They have to make Denver by tonight."

Pushing, pushing to keep that vacation on schedule.

"The other couple is going hiking in awhile. They'll leave the car here, and they're staying two more nights."

I told her I'd bring Rusty in after they'd left. We made our way inside during all this, and I got treated to hasty introductions, none of which I'd remember ten minutes from now.

"Let me help you clear up the breakfast dishes," I offered.

"You don't have to do that," she protested.

"I know, but I want to. I'm at the point where if I sit down I'll sleep for about a day. I really need to keep moving."

She looked like she might insist that I just lie down, but I didn't give her the chance. Heading straight for the dining room, I stacked plates and gathered glasses and silver. In the kitchen, I ran water in the sink, stacking the plates to soak. Mary sat at the kitchen table, tallying a bill for the departing guests.

"Just leave those dishes," she told me.

"I don't mind helping," I said.

"I know, but we can do them together after my people leave."

I picked up the place mats from the dining table and carried them to the back door to shake out the crumbs. Wiped off the table, set the centerpiece back in place, and made busy work tidying little things.

"Hey," Mary interrupted, "come on, you don't have to do all that. Let Rusty out of the car and let's go sit down. Everyone's gone now."

Overjoyed at being let out of the car, Rusty bounded around the perimeter of Mary's neat lawn a few times, joining with her dogs in some kind of tag game that only they understood. Mary and I went back inside and flopped on the plaid couches in the living room.

"Now, you going to fill me in?" she inquired.

I did, a brief version, ending with my night in jail.

She chuckled. "Now that's one privilege I haven't enjoyed myself," she said.

"I *know* someone at that clinic was the person who broke into my room at the motel," I insisted. "I just can't figure out why one of those doctors would be after me. The questions I've been asking around town shouldn't have prompted that."

"Well, you know with lawsuits what they are today," she said, "maybe they're scared of a malpractice suit. Even if Cynthia's death were Richard's fault, maybe the doctors are afraid they could somehow be held responsible."

I shrugged. It could make sense.

"Hey, it looks to me like you're about to doze off on me," she smiled. "Let's get your room made up and let you get some real sleep."

My eyelids felt like lead and my limbs were like rocks. She was right.

We went upstairs to the room Drake and I had shared, was it less than a week ago? The bed was rumpled and the bathroom felt humid from recent showers. Mary bustled about gathering the towels and replacing them with fresh ones from a drawer. She stripped the sheets from the bed in a couple of deft moves, balling them up and tossing them into a pile at the door.

"Here, we'll remake this real quick." She pulled clean sheets from a dresser drawer and quickly spread one. Flapping it toward me like a giant sail, she took one side and I took the other. Within two minutes, the bed was again smooth and inviting.

"Do you have stuff to bring in from the car?" she asked.

I went downstairs and retrieved my shopping bag. By the time I got back, she had spritzed disinfectant around the bathroom fixtures and wiped them off. There was no sign that the place had been recently vacated by other occupants.

"Now we'll cozy it up a little," she said, closing the white wood shutters, "and I'll try to keep everyone quiet. You sleep as long as you want — you need it." She closed the door quietly behind her.

In the bathroom, I unwrapped my new toothbrush and tooth-paste. Having a clean mouth made me realize that the rest of me wasn't exactly pristine, so I did a very quick, very hot shower. Within ten minutes I lay between the cool sheets, my mind and body gone limp.

Little sounds dragged me into wakefulness from time to time, but as soon as I realized where I was, I allowed myself to drift back into a pleasant darkness. I dreamed, pleasant little scenes, some with Drake and myself doing some mundane little everyday thing together, some going back to my childhood. My parents were there and the house appeared just as it is today. The actions were nothing extraordinary, just daily routine. I stretched and lay between sleep and wakefulness for some time before thinking to find out what time it was.

The sun had cast striped shadows through the shutters, but they had faded now into a soft gold, telling me that it must be late afternoon. I got up, feeling completely refreshed, not foggy headed like I usually would after sleeping in the daytime. Slipped on a pair of shorts and T-shirt and brushed my teeth again.

Sometime during the day, Mary had slipped in and gathered my dirty clothes. They sat in a neatly folded clean pile on the dresser. When I opened the door leading to the hall, Rusty raised his head. He'd been sleeping like a quiet sentinel outside my room.

"Hey, kid," I said, rubbing his ears vigorously.

He whapped his tail against the doorjamb, leaning into my legs, obviously relieved to see that I was okay.

Downstairs, Mary dozed on the living room couch, her head slightly back, her open mouth snoring softly. I tiptoed toward the wonderful smell emanating from the kitchen. Two large kettles simmered on the stove. Lifting the lids revealed one pot of pinto beans with plenty of ham and onion. The other contained green chile sauce, rich with chunks of beef and spices. My stomach rumbled in response. I helped myself to an apple from the fridge and walked softly back to the living room. Just as I reached one of the overstuffed chairs, a floor board creaked, bringing Mary slowly from her sleep.

"Welcome back," she smiled at me.

"Boy, I needed that," I agreed. "Between having very little sleep last night and the fright of my life the night before, I guess I've been stressed."

She nodded knowingly.

I told her about the carefree dreams I'd had during my long rest. "Guess that means I needed to put all this behind me for awhile."

"That's what we're here for," she said, "to give people a chance to unwind. It's amazing how many folks still can't do it, though. You know, they get up here at altitude where they should just veg out, but they don't. Always got that schedule to keep."

"Will your other guests be here for dinner?" I asked.

She glanced at her watch. "It's nearly five," she said. "They ought to be back soon. I always get a little worried with hikers who stay out too late. Had a pair of teenagers last summer didn't come back by dark. We had to call out Search and Rescue."

"The chile and beans sure smell good," I told her.

Almost in answer to her concern, we heard voices out in the yard. She got up and looked out the window. "Here they are now, thank goodness. Bet they'll be tired tonight."

As it turned out, the hikers were the energetic sort. They wanted quick showers, a change of clothes, and then decided to head into town for dinner. Mary and I dined by ourselves on the chile and beans. Afterward, she built a cozy fire and we nestled into the couches.

"So, what's going to happen next with your case?" she asked.

"Steve Bradley wants me to stay around for a couple of days. Says the judge will have to determine a fine for my breaking the lights at the clinic. Guess that was a stupid thing to do," I told her.

"Well, yeah," she agreed. "Why were you trying to get in there anyway?"

I briefly told her how I hoped to find something in the patient files that would lend a clue to Cynthia's death and to the over large number of miscarriages that seemed to affect women in the county.

"What kind of clue?" she asked.

"I don't know — the abusive husband might have been the culprit in Cynthia's case. I'd just hate to think a doctor would protect someone like that."

"You know there's been Phillips's in this town for a long time. Those boys' grandaddy and great-grandaddy were prominent businessmen here."

I remembered the old pictures in the miner's museum. There had been a building called Phillips Mercantile in one of them.

"I'll bet those were exciting times," I remarked, "with the mines going strong. The Hispanics and Indians that had been in these parts for a long time must have felt rather displaced."

"They worked in the mines, too, you know. Made real good wages for the times."

"Maybe I'll go back to that old museum tomorrow," I said. "Gotta have something to do with the whole day." I set my wine glass down on the coffee table and yawned. "Maybe the mountain air is getting to me," I told Mary. "I can't believe it but I'm already drifting back off to sleep."

"Well, why don't you just hit it for the night?" she said. "You need to catch up."

I didn't need to be told twice. Ten-thirty and I was feeling like I'd put in a full day. Rusty tagged along behind me as we went up the stairs.

26

Chattering birds caught my attention. Sunlight streamed through the slats in the shutters. I stretched once then got up to look out. The green lawn glistened with dewy sparkles. Rusty rose and pressed his nose to the door. I tiptoed over and opened it for him, certain that Mary would let him outside.

Back at the window, I watched him scamper across the lawn with the other dogs. I slid the window open and breathed the clean air. Except for the faint clinking of dishes in the kitchen and the bird's steady chatter, the world was silent. In the city, there's a perpetual background noise. I never realized how pervasive it was until I came here. For the first time since Drake left, I allowed myself to feel at peace.

A few minutes under the hot shower invigorated me and I put on my clean shorts and shirt before going downstairs to find Mary. She stood at the stove, scrambling eggs. A platter of crisp bacon waited under the warming hood and a sheet of golden-topped biscuits sat on the counter top.

"Hey," she greeted. "You look a hundred percent better than yesterday."

"I feel a million percent better," I assured her.

"Our hikers have already hit the trail," she said. "They sure are the restless sort. They took biscuits and bacon with them, so the rest is for us."

She scooped the thickened eggs onto two plates.

"Grab some flatware," she said, "and we can eat here in the kitchen. Unless you'd rather go in the dining room."

"Nope, kitchen's fine with me."

She stacked several biscuits in a cloth-lined wicker basket, carrying it and the bacon platter to the table. Butter and jam waited there already. I picked up the plates and set them down on the checkered cloth.

"What's your plan for the day?" she asked.

"Well, I thought I might go back to the miner's museum and look around. And maybe the newspaper office to look at old issues."

I didn't mention the miscarriage statistics I'd seen in Albuquerque, which I hoped to verify, corroborate, or somehow explain locally.

"Would it be okay if Rusty stays here while I go into town?" I asked after we'd put away all the eggs and a good-sized portion of the bacon and biscuits.

"No problem." We carried our plates to the sink and I put the leftover food away for her.

The road into town was dusty dry once again, all trace of the recent rain gone now. The day was clear although the temperature had dropped pleasantly from last week's highs. I drove slowly, savoring the pine-scented air, noticing little details like the colorful flowers along the roadside and the cool stream that crossed under the road.

In town, the air felt warm and much stuffier than in the mountains. The brown adobes contrasted sharply with the deep blue sky. Heat waves wriggled above the highway. The newspaper office was at the north end of town, about a block off the main road in an adobe building that might have once been a private residence. I pulled into the yard and parked in the dirt lot, taking the last of the approximately three spaces. The other two cars were middle-aged compacts of nondescript colors.

Inside, a twenty-something girl sat at a desk near the door, her eyes intent on a computer screen, her hand guiding the mouse attachment around a purple pad. On screen there appeared the layout of newspaper columns with blanks where the photos would go. She clicked a couple of times before acknowledging me.

"May I help you?" she finally asked.

I told her I'd like to look at back issues. She nodded and motioned me to follow her. I expected to find a microfiche reader and film but instead she led me into an alcove off the hall that contained a built-in Formica desk with shelves rising to the ceiling. The shelves contained bound copies of past papers.

"How far back do these go?" I asked.

"Um, like probably thirty years," she said, her eyes darting up to the shelves.

"And before that?"

She looked at me like I must be seriously deranged. "Older than thirty years?"

"Yes . . . there *was* a newspaper here way back then, wasn't there?"

"Well, yeah, I guess. The masthead says 1886."

"Are the older ones stored somewhere else?" I asked, determined to be as large a pain in the ass as I could be.

"I'd have to check. I've only worked here, like, about two years. I think I heard there was a fire once, a long time ago."

"I'd appreciate it if you would ask," I told her.

She left me alone with the bound papers, the desk, and an unpadded wooden chair. I scanned the spines, determining that each oversized book contained a year's worth of the small weekly paper. I pulled the most recent one, which ended with the December 31 issue of last year, now seven months old. I paged through to the Births and Deaths section.

One death, Thomas J. "Buck" Miller, aged eighty-nine. No births that week. Next paper, one birth, no deaths. Next paper. I got pretty quick at it and covered the entire year in about fifteen minutes. I tried to remember whether I'd read anything remarkable, but it seemed pretty average.

"I checked with Mr. Sargeant," the receptionist-reporter-computer person told me. "The really old copies of the paper are in the room across the hall. You can just go in there if you want."

She indicated the door and opened it for me, reaching around the edge of the wall to flip a light switch. I thanked her and she went back to her desk. I sampled another year, the next most recent one, but the lure of the old papers kept tugging at me. I glanced up and down the hall then ducked into the other room.

The room was obviously a catch-all for everything that needed storing. Boxes and papers filled every spare corner. Shelves filled with oversized books lined the walls. The bindings started out to be leather with hand tooled designs and gold stamped letters. They gradually evolved to vinyl and cardboard, like the ones in the hall alcove. Just to get a sense of things, I chose the oldest book. Opened the front cover. The Phillipsburg Gazette.

Phillipsburg.

As in named for the Phillips family. As in Doctors Rodney and Evan Phillips.

My brain wheeled into motion. I scanned the lead stories for the first several issues. The newspaper had been started by a Phillips. The Mercantile store was owned by a Phillips. The mayor was a Phillips, the town doctor, the assayer. I shoved the first volume back onto the shelf and pulled down another. Same story, second chapter.

Book after book came down from the shelves. The format stayed the same through the 1800s and into the roaring twenties. The Depression years passed with Phillips's in charge. The war began. Several Phillips men died heroically, according to their grandfather's newspaper. The 1950s brought prosperity to Phillipsburg, along with the rest of the country. Other family names appeared often enough that I was beginning to feel comfortable with them. Martinez, Romero, Smith, Hazelton, Baca, Torres. Evan Phillips birth was announced and well documented in photos.

In 1960, a man named Ben Torres ran for the state legislature. He must have run a vicious campaign, although only a fraction of his words made the newspaper. Evan Phillips' mother died and his father remarried. The late Mrs. Phillips had owned the newspaper. Within a short time, her stock was bought up by a corporation from Santa Fe. The Phillips family lost control, for the first time in the town's recorded history, of the news the town would read.

Ben Torres, the recently elected state Senator, introduced a bill in the state legislature to change the town's name from Phillipsburg back to its original Valle Escondido — Hidden Valley. The largely Hispanic New Mexico state legislature voted in the change with no objection and with no consulting the Phillips family. It was the end of an era.

My skin suddenly felt cold. Evan Phillips was a young child when this happened. Rodney was born to the second wife and probably wouldn't remember any of it. But their father must have been a very bitter man. Losing the power the family had once held over the little town must have rankled deeply. He probably ranted and railed against the Hispanics in the town. The young boys had probably been brainwashed with enough hateful prejudice to corrupt them forever.

I returned to the alcove to look again at the most recent newspapers. Something niggled at the back of my mind. I reread the birth records. Only one Hispanic baby had been born to a Valle Escondido family in the past six months, and that one had been delivered in the hospital in Santa Fe. I now knew what they were doing. I just had to find out how.

27

Near the plaza, I parked in the shade of a young mimosa tree about a half block from the museum.

The same old man sat behind the counter inside, perched on his wooden stool. He straightened some postcards and rearranged the booklets and tourism department freebies for my benefit. I paid the two dollar admission once again and walked into the room with all the old photos. It took me a few minutes to remember which one showed the Phillips Mercantile building. I wasn't positive, but thought the building still existed on the plaza. I memorized the shape of it, hoping to find out its current purpose.

Although the museum was small, I took my time covering it, making sure I absorbed all the information I could. Now that I was looking for it, the Phillips family name appeared with generous frequency. I recognized many of the photos from the newspaper accounts. Businesses owned by various Phillips's had been featured in news stories. The Phillips family home was pictured as a large adobe structure, not lavish by today's standards, but it dwarfed the other buildings around it at the time. I wondered if it still stood.

The museum's volunteer watchdog sat dozing precariously on his wooden stool. I scooted my feet a little, creating a gentle sound to waken him. He snorted back a snore and his head snapped up. I pretended I hadn't noticed.

"Could you tell me if the old Phillips home is still standing?" I asked. "The one shown in the pictures?"

He blinked two or three times. The wrinkles around his eyes deepened as he squinted in thought. Grizzled whiskers became more visible on his prominent chin. He worked his mouth in a chewing kind of motion, the better to get his memory working.

"Hmm, yup, I reckon so," he drawled from the side of his mouth. "Don't know that you'd recognize it, though. Place went way down hill after old man Phillips died."

"So none of the Phillips family live there now?" I asked.

"Hmph." It was more of a grunt than a word. "You can go see fer yerself," he said. "The place is out about three miles from town. Take County Road 12 east."

I thanked him and left, wondering whether it was really worth the trip. I had no reason to disbelieve the old man. Something told me the current Phillips's would live in modern places with lots of angles and skylights. My thoughts reverted back to the stories I'd seen in the old newspapers as I started my car and headed toward County Road 12.

The old adobe was so rundown that I drove by it twice before realizing it was the house I'd seen in the pictures. The upper story sagged, like an old woman bent by osteoporosis, her aged shoulders unable to bear the roof's weight any longer. The traditional territorial blue paint around the window and door frames had chipped away, leaving weathered gray wood with only tiny flecks of the blue intact. A wooden balcony had once been attached to the front, outside an upper story door. It drooped, only a couple of the wooden rungs still in place. The weight of a pigeon could possibly dislodge the whole thing.

In the yard, wild native plants had taken over where rock-bordered flower beds must have once been cultivated. A dozen or so stalks of hollyhock held their pink and fuchsia heads high. They dotted the yard randomly, the obvious product of flora left to its own devices. Two crumbling adobe pillars flanked the driveway entrance. From one of them hung a weathered sign: C. Sisneros, Artist. I couldn't see any indication that the artist was still in residence.

Some of the multi-paned windows were shattered, leaving the entire place looking sad and abandoned. Had Sisneros been the one to take the old homestead from the Phillips brothers? Or had that happened at some previous time in history? My brain struggled to put it all together.

Somehow I had to figure out exactly what was going on. I knew that somehow the two doctors were involved in the startling number of miscarriages in the small town, but how were they doing it? I thought of the third doctor in the practice, Brent Fisher. Sally had told me that he was new in town. He might not be so tightly wrapped up in old history. I headed back to town.

I stopped at a pay phone beside a gas station. Chris answered the phone at the clinic. I hoped she wouldn't recognize my voice.

"Yes, ma'am," I said, making my voice as nasal as possible, "which doctors are on duty this afternoon?"

"Well," she hesitated, "Doctor Evan Phillips is here now, but he's leaving at noon. Doctor Fisher will be in this afternoon. Can I make an appointment for you?"

"I'll call back," I said, hanging up before she had time to question further.

I drove toward the clinic, windows down against the warm day. Across the street and down perhaps a half block was a drive-in burger place. I parked where I could watch the clinic's parking lot and ordered a fresh lemonade through the crackly speaker beside my window. A carhop brought the drink. I stared at the cars across the street.

Within fifteen minutes, a dark blue sports car rushed into the clinic lot, chirping to a stop beside the building. Brent Fisher got out, unfolding his long legs and straightening his tie as he stood up. He pulled a briefcase from the car with one hand and smoothed his hair with the other. I watched him walk toward the front door.

He disappeared inside and I checked my watch. Twelve o'clock exactly. Within ten minutes, while I slowly sipped my lemonade, Dr. Phillips emerged from the clinic. He strode purposefully toward a dark Suburban, got in and started it without hesitation. I started my car as soon as he passed the drive-in without looking my way.

"Chris, I need to talk to Doctor Fisher. Real quick? Before his first patient comes in?"

"Well . . . I . . ."

"His office is right back here, isn't it?" I pushed through the double doors.

"Wait a second," she protested, "I better page him." She was picking up the phone, but I walked on in.

Doctor Fisher stood in his office with one arm in his jacket sleeve, the other out, holding the phone to his ear. He'd obviously been in the process of taking off the coat to change into a lab jacket when Chris paged him. I walked into the office and closed the door behind me before he quite figured out what was happening.

"It's . . . uh, okay, Chris. No, don't bother." He slowly replaced the receiver. "What do you want?"

"Please," I said, my voice non-threatening. "I just need to ask some questions and I think you're the only one I can talk to."

"This isn't medical, is it?" he queried. His eyes narrowed as he slipped the jacket off and hung it on the coat rack in the corner.

"You're the one who broke into the clinic the other night, aren't you?"

"Well, I never got in," I rushed to say. "It really was a dumb thing to do and I should have just come and asked some questions first."

"So you want me to put in the good word and tell them you didn't really mean it so they won't press charges?" His look told me not to even consider it.

"No, I guess I have to answer for that one myself. I wanted to ask you about something else. Look, I'm really putting myself on the line here, trusting that you won't run straight to either Doctor Phillips with this."

"Sit down," he said, his forehead wrinkled with puzzlement. He had already taken his seat behind the desk.

I briefly filled him in on the miscarriage statistics I'd read. I mentioned the town history I'd read in the old newspapers.

"Phillipsburg? I'd never heard that before," he said.

"I don't know," I admitted, "this could be pretty far-fetched, but I just have a gut feeling that somehow the Phillips family is tied into this. But think about it — the family lost its control in this town because of Hispanics. Their father probably drilled hatred into them. Now they're systematically wiping out the Hispanic population of this town. I mean, these women are their patients. Imagine the degree of control they exert here."

His look was frankly skeptical. "I think you're pretty far off base," he said. "I just cannot imagine either of the doctors being involved in something like this. You actually think they are causing women to lose their babies?"

"Well?"

"Without the women being the least bit suspicious? Miss Parker, I really do think you need a better grasp on reality. Look, I've got patients waiting."

He stood, indicating that the conversation was over. Pulling his white lab coat on, he ushered me out of the office with a firm hand on my back. I headed toward the double doors leading to the lobby, while he walked to one of the examination rooms and pulled a patient chart from a rack beside the door. From another exam room, I heard Chris's voice assuring someone that the doctor would be there shortly. I made a snap decision.

A linen closet opened onto an adjacent hallway and I ducked into it, seconds before Chris passed by on her way back to her desk. Knowing they were both temporarily occupied, I felt around on the wall for a light switch.

The tiny room was lined with shelves, neatly filled with cloth drapes and gowns and precisely labeled boxes of cotton balls, tongue depressors, and other medical supplies. In one corner of the floor sat a large canvas bag with drawstring top, about one-quarter full of used linens ready to be sent to the laundry. I dumped the contents and stashed them on an empty shelf, saving the canvas bag as a hiding place should I need one.

What on earth was I doing here? I should be going to Steve Bradley with my suspicions and let him do the followup. But somehow I knew he wouldn't. He didn't really believe a crime had been committed, much less did he have any interest in pinning it on the town's two most prominent citizens. I would have to come up with some evidence before he'd believe me.

And the only way I could think of to do that was to get a peek at the patient files. I pulled the canvas laundry bag near the door and switched off the light. I stepped into the bag, dropping my purse into the bottom of it and pulling the bag up as high as I could. It came nearly to my waist. If I crouched down, I thought it could be pulled up high enough to cover me. I prayed that I could make myself resemble rags.

I sat down, the loose bag draped around my lower half, my ears trained to the door for sounds. There was a steady stream of traffic up and down the main hall: patients coming and going, usually led by Chris, sometimes by Fisher himself. I was beginning to relax in my little hiding place, even dozed off for awhile. I awoke with a start, remembering my Jeep parked outside.

28

My plan, loosely, was to wait in my hiding place until closing time, then search the clinic at my leisure after everyone had left. But once Chris and the doctor were ready to go, wouldn't they realize that there was still a car outside? Even if they didn't immediately connect it to me, they would surely question its presence.

My fuzzy sleep-coated brain tried to think back to noon. I remembered driving over and parking. I had left the Jeep near the edge of the parking area, purposely as far from the doctor's sharp blue sports car as possible. There was a chance, maybe a small one, that they would assume my vehicle was parked at the business next door. Meanwhile, the large lemonade had worked its way through my system and I desperately needed to pee.

I groped around in my purse and found my keychain with the tiny flashlight attached. Pushed the button and got a dime-sized circle of light, enough to read my watch by. Four o'clock. My legs ached so badly I wasn't sure they would ever function correctly again. I debated about trying to stand up, wondered if there were any urine specimen bottles in the room. Pictured myself trying to accomplish the act and decided I could hold it.

I stood in place for a couple of minutes, letting the circulation return to my legs. A voice just outside the door shocked me into action.

"We have more swabs here in the closet, Doctor," Chris's voice said.

I ducked down, pulling the laundry bag over myself.

The doorknob rattled. A sliver of light from the hall sliced across the darkness.

"Oh, did you find more? Okay." The door closed.

My heart stopped slamming against my ribs and my breathing returned about five minutes later. What is it they say about surveillance work? Hours of boredom punctuated by moments of sheer terror. I leaned against the wall again for support.

Time dragged by and I checked my watch again. Fifteen minutes had passed. My mind began to wander aimlessly, like a child lost in the desert. Thoughts bounced around in my skull. Rusty. At Mary's. Drake. Home again? Ron. Did he know where I'd come? My ankles cramped. I flexed them. I dozed again.

Voices drifted from the hall sharpening and waning in the ebb and flow of traffic between the examining rooms. Occasional words came through but it was mostly a haze of noise, up and down in intensity. At some point, I became aware that the noise had faded. The whir of the air conditioning provided background, nothing more. My ears strained to catch other sounds. Five minutes passed with nothing. My bladder contracted painfully. I found my small flashlight again and checked the time. Ten after six.

My knees crackled in protest as I stood. I pressed my ear to the door, listening for any sound. Nothing.

My heart rate picked up speed as I stepped from my protective sack. The doorknob turned silently in my hand, the door easing open just a crack. The fluorescent overhead lights in the hall were off, with only a nightlight glowing orangely at the end. I edged the door open a little farther. The doors to the examining rooms stood open, gray oblongs that let late afternoon light, muffled by closed mini-blinds, into the hall. I realized I'd been holding my breath.

I stepped into the open gray space, edging my way along the hall to the double doors. A look through the small round windows in them revealed that the reception area was empty. Chris's desk was neat and clear. A small night lamp glowed on an end table. I tiptoed back down the hall toward Fisher's office. It, too, was dark and empty. I used a restroom, risking the noise of flushing.

Now what?

I glanced into each of the rooms, looking for the files before I remembered that they were behind Chris's reception desk. The cabinets themselves were modern looking things, smooth across the front, built directly into the walls. Recessed grooves formed the handles and none of them had anything so crass as a label on the outside. I guessed at which to try.

The first drawer I pulled out yielded names in the A's. I paused a minute to think again what I was looking for. Cynthia Martinez. I moved to the middle of the wall. It took two more tries, but the Martinez's finally came up. How did Chris deal with this unlabelled system all day?

Cynthia's file contained a wealth of information, but it was all in doctor-scritch. I could pick out a word here and there but nothing that made any sense. Was bad handwriting a required course in medical school? I slipped the file back into its spot. Tried to think.

Laura Armijo. She'd had two miscarriages, she told me. Back to the A's. Pulling out the top drawer, I realized that I'd missed it again. The drawer appeared to be business files rather than patient's. Curiosity made me linger there.

Bank statements. That might be interesting reading. Paid invoices. Suppliers. Travel.

I reached for the Paid Invoices. Much can be learned about people and their activities by the way they spend their money. I spread the file on the open drawer. Flipped through mundane stuff from medical supply houses, the linen service, the phone company. Two phone calls to France last month. Interesting. No overseas calls the month before or, as I continued backward through the file, in the previous six months.

A credit card bill from seven months ago showed a charge for plane tickets and a two-night hotel stay in Paris back in December. The week before Christmas. An odd time to take a European vacation. And who on earth flew to Paris for two days and came right home? I closed the folder and slowly replaced it. My brain spun into gear as I figured out what I was looking for.

I closed the file drawers and rushed back down the hall to Evan Phillips's office. He would only keep this little secret in a place where Chris wouldn't accidentally find it.

His room was darker than the rest, the windows covered with heavy drapes. It was still light outside, although the sun had dropped low in the sky. A massive desk dominated the room, the high-backed executive chair behind it cocked at an angle, like the occupant had just stood up. A couple of patient files were neatly placed on one corner. A leather trimmed desk pad sat precisely centered, with a matching pen holder and other desk accessories placed neatly around its perimeter. Obviously, the man's personal habits were much neater than his handwriting.

Two upholstered chairs stood in front of the desk, places where patients probably sat awaiting either good or bad news. The pictures on the walls were tastefully done Southwestern landscapes featuring adobe houses and lots of chamisa. I saw no file or storage cabinets. In the dim room, I decided to risk a lamp.

The desk must be the place. I walked around it to access the drawers. The first two opened to reveal a few file folders. One lower drawer had a bottle of scotch hidden at the back. An upper drawer was jammed full of prescription drug samples, the kind the drug companies give out by the handfuls. I began to pull the little sample packets out, placing them on the desk.

The names on the packages were all unfamiliar to me, multi-syllabled medi-speak. I placed them in little groupings with matching packages together. At the very back of the drawer I found what I was looking for.

They weren't labelled. That would be far too dangerous. The small white aspirin-like tablets were loose in a plastic bag. I only recognized them for what they were because I'd seen an article in *Newsweek* within the past month. RU 486. The abortion pill.

Phillips must have been smuggling them in from France for at least three or four years. Goose bumps sprouted on the back of my neck.

"What the *hell* are you doing!" Evan Phillips filled the doorway, clenched fists raised against the doorjamb on either side, as if he were holding it up. His eyes bored into me.

My breath sucked in, refusing to escape. I lowered the plastic bag, dropping it back into the open drawer.

"Well?" he demanded. "I asked what you think you're doing."

"I . . . uh . . . " I couldn't think of a single plausible reason I could give for my being here.

His eyes dropped to the desk for the first time, taking in the open drawer and scattered drug packages. I glanced at them, tempted to straighten the mess I'd made.

Click.

I knew that sound. He released the safety and pointed the semi-automatic straight at me.

"Now, Miss Parker, if you can't provide me with an extremely reasonable explanation of what you're doing in my office, I'm going to have to call the police."

Oh, please do. I didn't want Bradley to have to arrest me again, but anything was preferable to having my brains blown out. I searched for some means of defense. My purse and Ron's gun were neatly sacked in the linen closet.

"Well?"

Stall for time, Charlie. "Genocide, Dr. Phillips."

He feigned an incredulous look.

"As horrible as it sounds, you had figured out a way to rid this town of its Hispanic population. Only thing is, you chose a really slow way of going about it." I mentally groped for a way to get to my gun. "What were you planning to do? Not allow any more Hispanic babies to be born, but what about those who already live here? Were you planning to start murdering them outright soon?"

He squirmed a little. "You don't have any proof of that."

"These pills should do it," I said, raising the plastic bag. "Tell me, how did you get the women to take these?"

He lowered the gun slightly. It was probably getting heavy. "A patient will do just about anything her doctor tells her to. Those pills look almost exactly like aspirin, acetaminophen, any number of mild painkillers."

Cynthia Martinez had told her co-workers she'd had a headache the morning of her final doctor's appointment.

"But the abortion drug has to be administered in several doses," I said.

"Two." He said it coldly.

"So you administer the first dose here in the office and then send the second home with them?"

He shook his head. "Far too imprecise. The timing is still critical. But there's always a way to get them in here for that second followup appointment."

"And you've been traveling to France to get these?"

His eyes narrowed; his mouth formed a firm straight line. "Not always." The clipped words signalled the end of the conversation.

The gun pointed stiffly at me again. I tried to make eye contact with Phillips, but he was geared into a spot somewhere about the middle of me. I realized with a shock that he was taking aim, squeezing the trigger firmly.

I dove.

My elbows jolted against the carpet in the leg space beneath the desk, taking skin off as I skidded. Shattering glass tinkled against the desk top as one of the framed pictures disintegrated. Through the open crawl space, I could see Phillips's legs. His feet took a couple of tentative steps, as though he were trying to decide whether he had hit me or not. In a minute, he would come close enough to verify it and I'd bet money that he'd have the gun trained on me. And I was a prisoner of the desk. I gathered my legs up under me, positioning myself to spring.

When I hit Evan Phillips's legs with my full weight, he fell backward, landing on his butt. The second gunshot went up, knocking plaster dust from the ceiling. My ears rang as the explosion rebounded throughout the small room.

I scrambled to my hands and knees, scanning the area for the pistol. Phillips had the wind knocked out of him. He stared at the ceiling where fine particles of dust still floated through the air. The gun wasn't in either of his hands. Not on the floor. I didn't wait around.

I half crawled, half ran for the linen closet. Thumping sounds behind me told me that he was getting up. I had to assume he had the gun in possession once again.

The closet. Which door was it? My head felt hollow, the gunshot sound still ringing through it. I risked a look backward. The soles of his shoes were visible through the half-open door. Obviously, he was searching the floor for the weapon. I had only seconds to get away.

No way I'd make it through the front door and to my car in time. I ducked into the small closet, groping in the dark for my bag. I yanked at the zipper and felt for the pistol. It was loaded,

I knew, and I forced my mind to slow down enough to remember the steps to chamber a round and flip the safety off.

Should I wait for Phillips or should I be the aggressor? Get myself cornered or face the decision to shoot first? Darkness would be an ally. I opted for the closet.

The tiny room was dark except for the shaft of gray light coming through the doorway. I pressed my back against the shelves away from the light and took a deep breath, willing my arms to become steady.

Phillips was coming down the hall, none too quietly. I heard him muttering under his breath as he checked each of the examining rooms. His shadow interrupted the slice of light in my hiding place. It went on by. My hands shook. The shadow came back.

He must have realized that the closet door shouldn't be open.

"You in here, Miss Parker?" he wheedled. "Crouching in the corner? Shakin' in your boots?"

I took a steadying breath, raised the gun. Would I have the nerve to actually kill him?

"I've still got my weapon, you know," he teased. "I'm gonna find you." The door edged slowly open.

I aimed for the spot where I thought his heart would be. If he had one.

He spotted me.

The picture went into slow motion.

His gun swung to point at me. A dozen thoughts sped through my brain. Take a breath, aim. Go for the heart? I shifted my aim slightly, toward his shoulder instead. Held steady, squeezed the trigger.

His eyes widened in horror as my shot took him by surprise. His gun skittered to the floor. He fell backward into the hall. I picked up his gun and pointed both the weapons at him. I wasn't sure whether I'd hit him or merely surprised the hell out of him.

The light in the hall was fading fast.

"Get up," I ordered.

He moaned and gripped his right shoulder with his left hand. The hand came away bloody.

"Get up," I repeated.

He pushed himself into a sitting position against the far wall, still holding the shoulder. Blood darkened a saucer-sized area of his sleeve. I walked slowly toward him, never letting the guns waver.

"Get to your feet," I said. "Now. We're going out to the reception desk and you're going to call 911."

"Fine with me," he grunted. "Let's get the police here, where they'll find that you've broken into my offices and shot me. I caught you trying to steal drugs and you pulled a gun on me. With your prior attempt to break in here, this ought to clench it."

The hesitation must have registered on my face. He found a new surge of energy and rose to his feet.

"That's right," he said, "we'll just get the police over here as quickly as we can." He switched on a light and began to drag himself toward the double doors.

Steve Bradley stood there with two deputies behind him and three pistols pointed toward us.

"Thank goodness you're here!" Phillips and I both said it at once.

29

"Put the guns down and move to the side," Bradley ordered. Phillips jumped to interrupt. "Chief, she broke . . ."

"Can it, doctor. We'll talk to *you* later." Bradley stooped down to pick up the pistols I'd laid on the floor. The two deputies were still keeping Phillips and me in their sights.

I looked at Bradley quizzically. On the face of it, with me holding two pistols and Evan Phillips bleeding, I should have been the one in trouble.

I was.

The deputies herded us out to separate patrol cars for the five minute ride to the station. The female officer, Luellen, took me into Bradley's office.

"Can I get you some water or something?" she asked. "The chief wants you to wait in here till he gets back. We put the other guy in the interrogation room."

I slumped into a hard wooden chair beside the desk. With the adrenaline gone, my muscles had lost their will to support my frame.

"Yes, water would be nice," I told Luellen.

She didn't leave me alone, but turned to a sideboard and poured water from a thermal pitcher into a clean glass.

"Where's my purse?" I asked.

"Chief Bradley stayed behind to check out the evidence at the scene," she told me. "I'm sure he'll find it and bring it back."

I wondered if he would find the incriminating pills. Had Phillips destroyed them before he came after me with the gun? Officer Luellen picked up a clipboard and asked questions, to which I mumbled responses. My head hurt and I didn't want to come up with answers. I laid my head on my folded arms on the desk. My eyelids began to feel heavy.

"Well, here's your bag." A thump on the desk startled me out of a brief nap. "You can go anytime."

Bradley stood above me, his tired eyes drooping at the corners.

"What happened?" I asked.

"Well, you were right about that guy," he said. "We got the evidence."

My head was up now, alert. "Well?" I prodded.

"Doctor Fisher came by here earlier. He basically confirmed what you'd told me. He said you came by the office this afternoon and questioned him about the two Doctor Phillips's. At first he didn't believe it, but he did some checking. Looked in a couple of the patient files."

"I tried that. Couldn't read a thing."

He crossed behind the desk and flopped heavily in his chair.

"Well, I guess those docs can read each other's writing, even though no one else can. Evidently, Phillips didn't put his crimes in writing, he's not that stupid, but he used a few key phrases in each suspicious case, and that told Fisher what he needed to know. He found a couple of baggies with these little white pills in them in Phillips's desk. He brought me one of them."

I touched the little bag he held up. It was identical to the one I'd found. I told him about my encounter with the doctor.

"Why didn't you just come here and tell me?" he asked.

My energy returned. "Didn't I already try that?" I demanded. "Didn't I come here with my suspicions and you basically blew me off?"

At least he had the grace to look embarrassed. He nodded concedingly. "You're right, I should have listened."

"I mean, once my car was sabotaged at Mary's that night, didn't that tell you that someone was worried? That I was getting close to someone around here?" My adrenaline source had rejuvenated itself. "Who did that job on my car anyway?"

"Okay, okay. Calm down. I said you could go. Rod Phillips did the car damage, and broke into your motel room, and it looks like both of them were in on the RU486 plot. I'm not sure what crimes we'll charge them with exactly, but we have them. You can go back home to that man of yours."

Drake. Suddenly I wished he was waiting at home for me. A partner to go home to would be nice. My partner. Ron. He would have received my cryptic message on the office answering machine and was probably driving himself crazy wondering about me right now.

Someone had driven my Jeep to the station for me. It waited outside. The sun was completely down now and the sky had turned to a deep turquoise blue, clear and smooth as a stone. Darkness would come gradually and fully within the hour. I breathed deeply of the clean soft air, letting it soothe my soul.

Mary McDonald's lights glowed a soft welcome. I pulled slowly into the drive and shut off the ignition. Cicadas chirped somewhere within the woods and an owl hoo'd softly. Something caught in my throat as Rusty bounded out to greet me.

"Hey, we were getting a little worried," Mary greeted, following closely behind Rusty. She wrapped her arms around me as I stepped from the car. "You look toasted."

"I nearly was," I said tiredly. "I need to make a couple of calls."

"Sure, sure. You come right in and let me make you a cup of tea."

I dialed Ron's number first.

"Where the hell are you?" He nearly shouted the words.

"Hey! Don't give me any shit right now." I breathed deeply and started over. "Ron, sorry, I'm fine. I'm in Valle Escondido and I'll be home in a couple of hours. I'll explain everything."

Drake's phone rang four times before he picked up.

"Hi, sweetheart, I've been thinking about you. Did you get my message?" His voice was deep and sweet and soothing.

"No, I haven't been home for a couple of days." I explained briefly, but decided I'd save the worst of it for later, after I'd put my thoughts together.

"Well, you take care of yourself," he said. "Make sure you eat your vegetables."

I smiled as we said goodbye.

"Here's your tea," Mary said. "You ought to take a hot bath and get to bed early."

Suddenly, more than anything, I wanted to be home. I wanted my own bed and I wanted my life to settle back into its old routine.

"I think I'll drive back tonight," I told Mary as we sipped our tea. "It's still early. I'll be home by ten."

Hadn't I said something similar to myself a couple of nights ago? Before I'd attempted the foolish break-in at the clinic. Before I'd discovered the horrible truth about Evan and Rodney Phillips.

The clock said nine thirty-seven when I pulled into my driveway. Rusty bounded out of the car, happy to be home. I carried my small bag and purse inside. The house felt like a strange place. I'd spent so little time there in recent weeks. I dumped my clothes in the hamper and bustled about watering houseplants and catching a few cobwebs with the duster.

There was one loose end I should take care of. It could be done in the morning at the office, but I was extremely tempted to take a couple of days off before going back.

I dialed Sally's number while I reached into the freezer for a carton of chocolate ice cream I'd left there over a week ago. She answered just as I was scooping the first spoonful into my mouth.

"Charlie? What is it?"

I filled her in on my findings in Valle Escondido.

"You might want to call Laura and let her know," I said. There was silence at the other end of the line as I devoured another spoonful of chocolate. "Sally? You okay?"

"It's just so horrible," she whispered. "I can't believe a doctor would do such a thing."

"I know. Sick behavior." I waited through a minute of silence on her end. "Sally? Listen, you aren't in any danger like that. You're going to be fine. Your baby is going to be fine."

We talked a few more minutes, until I felt reassured that she would be okay. I had eaten about half the ice cream and knew I'd better quit. I hung up the phone and headed for the kitchen. Rusty waited, reminding me that he had not had his dinner yet.

"Can you just wait till I put the ice cream away?" I teased.

I opened the freezer and set the carton back. Then I noticed the small blue box. Sitting on top of a package of green beans. *Eat your vegetables*, Drake had said. My breathing quickened.

The velveteen was cool with frost. I slowly raised the hinged lid. A tiny slip of paper fell into my hand.

Put this on whenever you're ready. I'll be waiting.

The diamond glittered like an exquisitely shaped ice crystal.